D0997301

• THE NEW WINDMILL BOOK OF •

Scottish Short Stories

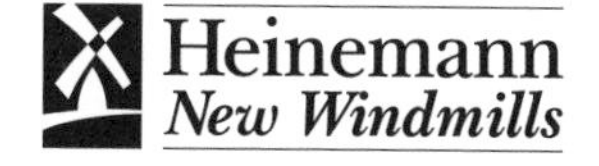
Heinemann
New Windmills

Heinemann Educational Publishers
Halley Court, Jordan Hill, Oxford OX2 8EJ
Part of Harcourt Education

Heinemann is the registered trademark of Harcourt Education Limited

4

ISBN: 978 0 435125 12 7

Acknowledgements
The Editor and Publishers would like to thank the following for permission to use copyright material:

Anne Donovan for 'All that Glisters', first published in Scotland on Sunday 1997, after winning the Macallan/Scotland on Sunday short story competition; Gillon Aitken Associates Ltd for 'The Only Only' by Candia McWilliam from *New Writing 3*, published by Minerva 1994. Copyright © Candia McWilliam 1994; Random House UK Ltd for 'All the Little Loved Ones' by Dilys Rose from *Red Tides*, published by Martin, Secker & Warburg; Random House UK Ltd for 'Fearless' by Janice Galloway from *Blood*, published by Martin, Secker and Warburg; Brian McCabe for 'Feathered Choristers' from *Scottish Short Stories*, published by William Coling; Matthew Fitt, Liz Neven and Pete Fortune at Watergaw for 'Striker' from *A Braw Brew*, published by Watergaw 1997; Sheil Land Associates Ltd for 'Rupert Bear and the San Izal' by Alan Spence from *Stone Garden and Other Stories*, published by Phoenix House; Lorn Macintyre for 'Saskatchewan' by Lorn Macintyre from *The Flamingo Book of New Scottish Writing 1998*; Sheila Douglas for 'The Haemcomin' by Sheila Douglas from *A Tongue in Yer Heid*, published by B & W Publishing; Audrey Evans for 'Mossy' by Audrey Evans from *Scottish Short Stories 1986*, published by William Collins; Carcanet Press Ltd for 'Napoleon and I' by Iain Crichton Smith from *Selected Stories 1990*, published by Carcanet Press Ltd; Bloomsbury Publishing Plc for 'The Lighthouse' from *People Like That*, by Agnes Owens, published by Bloomsbury Publishing Plc, 1996.

The Publishers have made every effort to trace the copyright holders, but if they have inadvertently overlooked any, they will be pleased to make the necessary arrangements at the first opportunity.

Cover design by The Point
Cover photographs by Tony Stone Images
Typeset by TA Tek-Art, Croydon, Surrey
Printed in China by CTPS

Contents

Key:

* = Intermediate 1

** = Intermediate 2

*** = Higher

Dedication

For Adrian and Anna

Acknowledgements

The editor wishes to thank Ann Bridges, Tricia Duncan and Kenny McIntosh for their invaluable support and advice.

Introduction

This collection of twelve Scottish short stories is designed for use with students working towards Intermediate 1, Intermediate 2 or Higher level English and Communication under the SQA Higher Still arrangements. An indication is given on the Contents page of a suggested level for each story, although teachers should use their own professional judgement and knowledge of their students to decide on the appropriateness of a text or texts.

The Literary Study (Unit Two) activities for each story are organised under the broad headings of *Understanding and Evaluation* and *Analysis*; these are designed for formative use only. In the *Understanding and Evaluation* section, the questions are intended to develop students' skills in understanding the story (Outcome 1 Performance Criteria – Understanding) and their personal engagement with it (Outcome 1 Performance Criteria – Evaluation). There follows an *Analysis* section which consists of an aspect of the short story, an extract from the text and questions directing students to a close reading of this extract (Outcome 1 Performance Criteria – Analysis). Certain of the *Analysis* questions will also involve students in evaluating the effectiveness of a particular aspect. In practice, these performance criteria are inter-related.

For each text, there is one suggested Group Discussion task and one suggested Individual Presentation task. Finally, two Writing suggestions are given. The Talking and Writing activities can be used formatively or summatively.

An integrated approach is useful in the study of these texts. For example, a Group Discussion on an important theme could provide a useful preliminary activity for a piece of Writing (as well as providing a formative or summative assessment opportunity for Unit 3B Group Discussion). In the same way, the analysis questions give useful formative practice for Textual Analysis but will also provide support for students in preparing Critical Essays.

For each story, one specific aspect of the text has been chosen for close analysis. Nevertheless, teachers should not feel constrained by this device and students should be encouraged to consider a number of different aspects of the text before a Critical Essay is attempted. For example, in 'Napoleon and I' consideration could be given to *relationships* and *narrative voice* as well as *description*. Similarly, one short extract has been chosen to illustrate a specific aspect but students should also be directed to other crucial areas of the text. The teacher may also wish to support students in moving from close textual analysis to extended critical writing by assigning shorter formative pieces of work on a number of aspects of a given story or pair of stories. There are Critical Essay questions, tailored to the anthology, at the end of the book.

Family

All that Glisters

Anne Donovan

Thon wee wifey brung them in, the wan that took us for two days when Mrs McDonald wis aff. She got us tae make Christmas cards wi coloured cardboard and felties, which wis a bit much when we're in second year, but naebdy wis gonny say anythin cos it wis better than daein real work. Anyway ah like daein things lik that and made a right neat wee card for ma daddy wi a Christmas tree and a robin and a bit a holly on it.

That's lovely dear. What's your name?

Clare.

Would you like to use the glitter pens?

And she pulled oot the pack fae her bag.

Ah'd never seen them afore. When ah wis in primary four the teacher gied us tubes of glitter but it wis quite messy, hauf the stuff ended up on the flair and it wis hard tae make sure you got the glue in the right places. But these pens were different cos the glue wis mixed in wi the glitter so you could jist draw with them. It wis pure brilliant so it wis. There wis four colours, rid, green, gold and silver, and it took a wee while tae get the hang of it. You had tae be careful when you squeezed the tube so's you didny get a big blob appearin at wanst, but efter a few goes ah wis up an runnin.

And when ah'd finished somethin amazin hud happened. Ah canny explain whit it wis but the glitter jist brought everythin tae life, gleamin and glisterin agin the flat cardboard. It wis like the difference between a Christmas tree skinklin wi fairy lights an wan lyin deid an daurk in a corner.

Ma daddy wis dead chuffed. He pit the card on the bedside table and smiled.

Fair brightens up this room, hen.

It's good tae find sumpn that cheers him up even a wee bit because ma daddy's really sick. He's had a cough fur as long as ah can remember, and he husny worked fur years, but these past three month he canny even get oot his bed. Ah hear him coughin in the night sometimes and it's different fae the way he used tae cough, comes fae deeper inside him somehow, seems tae rack his hale body fae inside oot. When ah come in fae school ah go and sit wi him and tell him aboot whit's happened that day, but hauf the time he looks away fae me and stares at a patch on the downie cover where there's a coffee stain that ma ma canny wash oot. He used tae work strippin oot buildins and he wis breathin in stour* aw day, sometimes it wis that bad he'd come hame wi his hair and his claes clartit* wi it. He used tae kid on he wis a ghost and walk in the hoose wi his airms stretched oot afore him and ah'd rin and hide unner the stair, watchin him walk by wi the faint powdery whiteness floatin roon his heid.

He never knew there wis asbestos in the dust, never knew a thing aboot it then, nane of them did. Noo he's an expert on it, read up aw these books tae try and unnerstaun it fur the compensation case. Before he got really sick he used tae talk aboot it sometimes.

You see, hen, the word asbestos comes fae a Greek word that means indestructible. That's how they use it fur fireproofin – the fire canny destroy it.

You mean if you wore an asbestos suit you could walk through fire and it widny hurt you?

Aye. In the aulden days they used tae bury the royals in it. They cried it the funeral dress of kings.

The next day the wee wumman let me use the pens again. Sometimes when you think somethin's brilliant it disny last, you get fed up wi it dead quick an don't know why you wanted it in the first place. But the pens wereny like that, it wis even better than the first time cos ah knew whit tae dae wi them. Yesterday ah'd put the glitter on quite thick in a solid block a colour, but today ah found a different way a daein it almost by accident. Ah'd drawn a leaf shape and coloured it green but a bit squirted oot intae a big blob, so ah blotted it and when ah took the paper away the shape that wis left wis nicer

---

*stour: dust

*clartit: fouled, dirty

than the wan ah'd made deliberately. The outline wis blurred and the glitter wis finer and lighter, the colour of the card showin through so it looked as if sumbdy'd sprinkled it, steidy* ladelin it on; it looked crackin. The teacher thought so too.

It's lovely, Clare. It's more . . . subtle.

Subtle, ah liked that word.

Ah tellt ma daddy aboot it that night efter school, sittin on the chair beside his bed. He seemed a bit better than usual, mair alert, listenin tae whit ah hud tae say, but his skin wis a terrible colour and his cheeks were hollow.

Whit did she mean, subtle, hen? How wis it subtle?

Ah tried tae think of the words tae explain it, but ah couldny. Ah looked at ma fingers which were covered in glitter glue and then at ma daddy's haun lyin on the bedcover, bones stickn oot and veins showin through. Ah took his haun in mines and turnt it roon so his palm faced upward.

Look, daddy.

Ah showed him the middle finger of ma right haun, which wis thick wi solid gold, then pressed doon on his palm. The imprint of ma finger left sparkly wee trails a light.

He smiled, a wavery wee smile.

Aye, hen. Subtle.

That night ah lay awake fur a while imaginin aw the things ah could dae wi the glitter pens. Ah really wanted tae make sumpn fur ma daddy's Christmas wi them. The tips of ma fingers were still covered in glitter, and they sparkled in the daurk. Ah pressed ma fingers aw ower the bedclothes so they gleamed in the light fae the streetlamps ootside, then ah fell intae a deep glistery sleep.

£3.49 for a pack of four. And ah hud wan ninety-three in ma purse.

Ah lifted the pack and walked to the check-oot.

Much are they?

Three forty-nine.

Aye but much are they each?

The wumman at the till hud dyed jet-black hair and nae eyebrows.

---

*steidy: instead of

We don't sell them individually.

She spat oot the word *individually* as if it wis sumpn disgusting.

Aye but you'll get mair fur them. Look, you can have wan ninety-three fur two.

Ah've already tellt you that we don't sell them individually, ah canny split the pack.

Ah could see there wis nae point in arguin wi her so ah turnt roon and walked towards the shelf tae pit them back. If Donna'd been wi me, she'd just have knocked them. She's aye takin sweeties an rubbers an wee things lik that. She's that casual aboot it, she can jist walk past a shelf and wheech sumpn intae her pocket afore anybdy notices, never gets caught. And she's that innocent lookin, wi her blonde frizzy curls an her neat school uniform naebdy wid guess tae look at her she wis a tea-leaf.

She's aye on tae me tae dae it, but ah canny. Ah suppose it's cos of ma ma and da, they're dead agin thievin. Donna widny rob hooses or steal sumpn oot yer purse but she disny think stealin oot a shop is stealin. A lot of folk think lik that. Donna's big brother Jimmy wanst tried tae explain tae me that it wis OK tae steal ooty shops cos they made such big profits that they were really stealin affy us (the workin classes he cries us though he husny worked a day in his life) and they're aw insured anyway so it disny matter, and even though ah can see the sense in whit Jimmy's sayin, well, ma daddy says stealin is stealin, and ah canny go against his word.

In the end ah sellt ma dinner tickets tae big Maggie Hughes and all week ah wis starvin for ah only hud an apple or a biscuit ma ma gied me fur a playpiece. But on Friday it wis worth it when ah went doon the shops at lunchtime tae buy the pens. It wis a different wumman that served me and she smiled as she pit them in a wee plastic poke.

Are you gonny make Christmas decorations, hen?

Ah'm no sure.

Ah got some fur ma wee boy an he loved them.

Aye they're dead good. Thanks.

*

Ah couldny wait tae show them tae ma da, but as soon as ah opened the door of the hoose ah knew there wis sumpn wrang. It wis that quiet, nae telly, nae radio on in the kitchen. Ma mammy wis sittin on the settee in the livinroom. Her face wis white and there were big black lines under her eyes.

Mammy, whit's . . . ?

C'mere hen, sit doon beside me.

She held her weddin ring between the thumb and first finger of her right haun, twistin it roon as she spoke and ah saw how loose it wis on her finger. No long ago it wis that tight she couldny get it aff.

Clare, yer daddy had a bad turn, jist this afternoon and we had tae go tae the hospital wi him. Ah'm awful sorry hen, ah don't know how tae tell you, but yer daddy's died.

Ah knew it wis comin, ah think ah'd known since ah walked intae the hoose, but when she said the words the coldness shot through me till ah felt ma bones shiverin and ah heard a voice, far away in anither room, shoutin but the shouts were muffled as if in a fog, and the voice wis shoutin *naw, naw, naw!*

And ah knew it wis ma voice.

We sat there, ma mammy and me, her airms roon me, till ah felt the warmth of her body gradually dissolve the ice of mine. Then she spoke, quiet and soft.

Now hen, you know that this is fur the best, no fur us but fur yer daddy.

Blue veins criss-crossed the back of her haun. Why were veins blue when blood wis red?

You know yer daddy'd no been well fur a long time. He wis in a lot of pain, and he wisny gonny get better. At least this way he didny suffer as much. He's at peace noo.

We sat for a long time, no speakin, just haudin hauns.

The funeral wis on the Wednesday and the days inbetween were a blur of folk comin an goin, of makin sandwiches and drinkin mugs of stewed tea, sayin rosaries an pourin oot glasses of whisky for men in overcoats. His body came hame tae the hoose and wis pit in their bedroom. Ma mammy slept in the bed settee in the livin room wi ma auntie Pauline.

Are you sure that you want tae see him?

Ah wis sure. Ah couldny bear the fact we'd never said goodbye and kept goin ower and ower in ma mind whit ah'd have said tae him if ah'd known he wis gonny die so soon. Ah wis feart as well, right enough. Ah'd never seen a deid body afore, and ah didny know whit tae expect, but he looked as if he wis asleep, better, in fact than he'd looked when he wis alive, his face had mair colour, wis less yella lookin an lined. Ah sat wi him fur a while in the room, no sayin anythin, no even thinkin really, jist sittin. Ah felt that his goin wis incomplete and ah wanted tae dae sumpn fur him, but that's daft, whit can you dae when sumbdy's deid? Ah wondered if ah should ask ma mammy but she wis that withdrawn intae hersel, so busy wi the arrangements that ah didny like tae. She still smiled at me but it wis a watery far-away smile and when she kissed me goodnight ah felt she wis haudin me away fae her.

On the Wednesday mornin ah got up early, got dressed and went through tae the kitchen. Ma auntie Pauline wis sittin at the table havin a cuppa tea and a fag and when she looked up her face froze over.

Whit the hell dae you think you're daein? Go and get changed this minute.

But these are ma best claes.

You canny wear red tae a funeral. You have tae show respect fur the deid.

But these were ma daddy's favourites. He said ah looked brilliant in this.

Ah mind his face when ah came intae the room a couple of month ago, after ma mammy'd bought me this outfit fur ma birthday; a red skirt and a zip-up jaicket wi red tights tae match.

You're a sight fur sore eyes, hen.

That sounds horrible, daddy.

He smiled at me.

It disny mean that hen, it means you look that nice that you would make sore eyes feel better. Gie's a twirl, princess.

And ah birled roon on wan leg, laughin.

They claes are no suitable for a funeral.

Ah'm gonny ask ma mammy.

Ah turned to go oot the room.

Don't you dare disturb your mother on a day like this tae ask her aboot claes. Have you no sense? Clare, you're no a baby, it's time you grew up and showed some consideration for other folk. Get back in that room and put on your school skirt and sweatshirt and your navy blue coat. And ah don't want to hear another word aboot this.

In the bedroom ah threw masel intae a corner and howled ma heid aff. The tears kept comin and comin till ah felt ah wis squeezed dry and would never be able tae shed anither tear. Ah took aff the red claes and changed intae ma grey school skirt and sweatshirt and pit ma navy blue coat ower it. Ah looked at masel in the full-length mirror in the middle of the wardrobe and saw this dull drab figure, skin aw peely-wally. My daddy would have hated tae see me like this but ah didny dare go against ma auntie's word.

The only bit of me that had any life aboot it wis ma eyes fur the tears had washed them clean and clear. A sunbeam came through the windae and ah watched the dustspecks dancin in its light. There was a hair on the collar of ma coat and it lit up intae a rainbow of colours. As ah picked it up and held it in ma fingers an idea came tae me. Ah went tae ma schoolbag which had been left lyin in the corner of the room since Friday, took oot ma pack of glitter pens and unwrapped them. Ah took the gold wan, squeezin the glitter on ma fingers then rubbin it intae ma hair, then added silver and red and green. The strands of hair stood oot roon ma heid like a halo, glisterin and dancin in the light. Ah covered the dull cloth so it wis bleezin wi light, patterns scattered across it, even pit some on ma tights and ma shoes. Then ah pressed ma glittery fingers on ma face, feelin ma cheek bones and eyebrows and the soft flesh of ma mouth and the delicate skin of ma eyelids. And ah felt sad for a moment as ah thought of the deid flesh of ma daddy, lyin alone in the cold church. Then ah stood and looked in the mirror at the glowin figure afore me and ah smiled.

Subtle, daddy?

Aye hen, subtle.

The Only Only

Candia McWilliam

The first ferry for a week was fast to the quay, the thick rope springs holding it to, looped fore and aft over iron cleats* the height of children. The weather had been so hard and high that there was seaweed all over the island, brought in by the wind, and the east wall of each house was drifted up to the roof. The children dug in to these drifts and made blue caves to sit in, smoothing till the cave's inner ice melted and set to a clear lucent* veneer.

Seven children lived on the island and attended the school together. Sandy was the only only among them; the rest had brothers or sisters. She was a girl of eight born to the teacher Euphemia and her husband Davie, who set and lifted lobsterpots for his main living, though the ferry company kept him on a retainer to attend the arrival and departure of the ferry, three times a week when the sea would let it through. Davie'd to hook up and untie the boat, watch for the embarkation of livestock and the safe operation of the davits* on the quay. He had an eye to the secure delivery of post and to the setting in place of the gangplank so that it would hold in a swell.

He liked his job. It involved him with everyone who lived on the island and he was careful to respect this. If he knew that the father of a child off just now inside its mother on the ferry to be born on the mainland was not the man with his arm around the woman as the ship parted from the land, he did not say. Davie was not an islander born, although Euphemia was; she could remember her grandmother skinning fulmars to salt them for the winter and she herself could feel if the egg of a gull might be taken for food or if it was fertilised and packed with

---

*cleats: pieces attached to a ship for fastening ropes
*lucent: light
*davits: hoists

affronted life. Davie had boiled up a clutch of eggs once and they had sat down to them with a salad and pink potatoes from outdoors; the tapping and the faint window of membrane had seemed right enough, but when he'd got through to the boiled halfmade chick with its eggtooth sticking out like a sail needle's hook, he'd got sick. He still looked away when a seal heaved up the rocks to die after a gashing; the thickness of the blubber inside gave him a lurch, like seeing the legs above an old woman's stocking tops. In death a seal keeps its enthusiastic expression; the human face falls to neutral peace, but the seal appears to trust even death.

Because there had been no boat for some time, everyone was on the pier today. It was a social occasion although it was so cold. Something seemed to have slowed the sea, its salt particles surrendering to the grip ice has on water. On the Atlantic coast of the island, rockpools were freezing over, the crabs moving in under sea lettuce to escape seizure by the ice. Among the blue-brown mussels that clustered around the stanchions* of the pier hung icicles at low tide. The sea was unusually quiet, hushed by the cold from lapping or thrashing the shingle or the harbour walls. Only the hardiest boats were still down in the water, fishing boats and a clam skiff that had been neglected and had taken in water that was now a hard slope of grey ice halfway up to the gunwales.

On the slip where the smaller boats came alongside there was a tangle of nets and a pile of polythene fishboxes. Yellow, orange, mauve and electric blue, the nets were neatly trimmed with a white buzz of rime*. The impression of a deserted, frozen harlequinade was emphasised by a pair of red heavy-duty gloves lying on the weed next to a single yellow seaboot.

Sandy stood with Euphemia in a group of women. People asked the teacher about their children; in such a community there was no chance of going unnoticed. Talk was the pastime, talk and work the currency. Euphemia was pleased to be among women, with her daughter. When, as now, she was irked at her

---

*stanchions: upright supports
*rime: frost

man she did not tell, or it would have been round the place before tea.

She wanted him to give up the boat and come into teaching at the school with her. She could not see the future in working on the pier. It took up a good day three times a week, when the following up had been done, the cargo counted, the letters sorted and settled in the red Land Rover to be taken round the only road by the post; and by the time drink had been taken, with the purser maybe, or with whoever came off the boat or was in the bar off a fishing boat.

He was a good man, but where did these boat days go? Whereas, should he come in with her at the teaching, they would see their work as it grew day by day. And he could still do the lobsters, if there were any left in the sea. With the French and the Russians and the warm-water breeders at it, the sea was full of mostly red herrings, forget the silver darlings.

Sandy now, she would see more of her father if he came in with the teaching, and then Euphemia maybe, when it was all settled, would get down to having another baby.

The purple line at the horizon lay over the slow grey sea. The air smelt of weed, cigarettes and diesel; the post office van was idling and the men gathered around it in their oilskins, smoking for the warmth. The children of the island were standing against the rail at the end of the pier, their feet kicking against the robust wire barrier with a bright harsh chiming. Six of them red-headed, in shades of red from orangeade to a bracken mixed with rough briar brown, and one of them with the crow-black hair that does not shine and goes with blue eyes. The children were waiting to wave, even those who were waving no one off; it was the boat, which was the presiding event of their lives, that they wished to acknowledge.

Against the folding evening clouds, and frosted by their departing rims of hard light, the shining ruby-juice red of Sandy's straight hair and the drained white of her face seemed to Euphemia to be stamped like a royal seal set to important words. It was not easy to think of Sandy with a brother or a sister. But Euphemia did not approve of only children; especially not here, where circumstances were already isolated in the world's eyes. It was not possible to imagine loving Sandy any less or loving any child more than Sandy was loved; it was hard to imagine the love that Davie and she bore for their child stretching to accommodate more, but Euphemia was convinced that this would occur naturally, without pain, like passing through a door into a new room with open windows.

The ferry was loaded. The gangplank was lifted on its ropes and let down to the pier for rolling and storage in the metal waiting room at the end where the children hung and bobbed and cuffed one another's bright heads. A long plaintive blast warned that the boat must soon go and the children hollered back to it through cupped hands. Lights were coming on in the boat; soon the dark would land over them all, steaming across the water from the purple edge of the sea.

Davie was checking that goods had been properly exchanged, the gangmower sent to the mainland for fixing by June time, the cowcake fetched up out of the hold, the canned goods and frozen gear stowed ready for the shop, the box of specially requested medicaments boxed up for the doctor, the beer rolled into the pub's Bedford van; detail was what mattered in this job, and he took a pride in it.

In the restful numbed cold silence, people began to prepare themselves to make farewell and to depart for their homes. The moment the children loved was coming, when they could wave to the boat as it pulled out and away from the island, seagulls over the wake like bridesmaids. They stood and waited at the pier end, looking out to sea.

There was a creak, a sodden tugging groaning. The seagulls gathered. The eighty people on the pier experienced the shared illusion that it was they and not the boat who moved. The rudder of the ship was churning deep under the water which, astern, showed silvery green below its surface and white above. The air was still enough for a hundred separate lifted voices to reach the ears intended as the twenty souls on the boat looked down to the crowd on the pier. The children waited.

The stern spring of the boat cracked free of the cleat from which Davie had forgotten to lift it. After the first tearing report of the bust rope came the whipping weight of sixty yards of corded hemp and steel, swinging out through its hard blind arc at the height of a good-sized child.

'Lie down, get down, for God's sake,' yelled a man. The women fell to the ground. Unless they were mothers, when they ran for their little ones to the end of the pier as the thick murderous rope lashed out, rigid and determined as a scythe to cut down all that stood in its way.

Sandy lay under her mother's heart, hearing it in the coat that covered them both. The concrete of the pier seemed to tremble with the hard commotion of the rope's passing over them.

Snapped out of her dreams, Euphemia held her only child.

The boat continued to move away, its briefly lethal rope trailing behind it, a lone seaman at the winch above, coiling it in to usefulness. The black ferrous patina* on the big cleat had burned off under the seething tension of the rope; its stem was polished by force through to a pale refined metal blue. The children from the end of the pier comforted their mothers, who stared out to the disappearing ship seeing, abob in the water, the heads of children cut off at the neck, their frozen sweetness of face under the streaming curtailed hair; red, red, red, red, red, red or black, and to grow no more.

---

*ferrous patina: iron oxide coating

All The Little Loved Ones

Dilys Rose

I love my kids. My husband too, though sometimes he asks me whether I do; asks the question. Do you still love me? He asks it while I am in the middle of rinsing spinach or loading washing into the machine, or chasing a trail of toys across the kitchen floor. When he asks the question at a time like this it's like he's speaking an ancient, forgotten language. I can remember a few isolated words but can't connect them, can't get the gist, don't know how to answer. Of course I could say, Yes I love you, still love you, of course I still love you. If I didn't still love you I wouldn't be here, would I, wouldn't have hung around just to go through the motions of companionship and sex. Being alone never bothered me. It was something I chose. Before I chose you. But of course that is not accurate. Once you become a parent there is no longer a simple equation.

We have three children. All our own. Blood of our blood, flesh of our flesh etc., delivered into our hands in the usual way, a slithering mess of blood and slime and wonder, another tiny miracle.

In reply to the question my husband doesn't want to hear any of my irritating justifications for sticking around, my caustic logic. He doesn't really want to hear anything at all. The response he wants is a visual and tactile one. He wants me to drop the spinach, the laundry, the toys, sweep my hair out of my eyes, turn round, away from what I'm doing and look at him, look lovingly into his dark, demanding eyes, walk across the kitchen floor – which needs to be swept again – stand over him as he sits at the table fingering a daffodil, still bright in its fluted centre but crisp and brown at the edges, as if it's been singed. My husband wants me to cuddle up close.

Sometimes I can do it, the right thing, what's needed. Other times, when I hear those words it's like I've been turned to marble or ice, to something cold and hard and unyielding. I can't even turn my head away from the sink, far less walk those few steps across the floor. I can't even think about it. And when he asks, What are you thinking? Again I'm stuck. Does it count as thinking to be considering whether there is time to bring down the laundry from the pulley to make room for the next load before I shake off the rinsing water, pat the leaves dry, chop off the stalks and spin the green stuff around the Magimix? That's usually what my mind is doing, that is its activity and if it can be called thinking, then that's what I'm doing. Thinking about something not worth relating.

– What are you thinking?

– Nothing. I'm not thinking about anything.

Which isn't the same thing. Thinking about nothing means mental activity, a focusing of the mind on the fact or idea of nothing and that's not what I'm doing. I've no interest in that kind of activity, no time for it, no time to ponder the true meaning of life, the essential nature of the universe and so on. Such speculation is beyond me. Usually when I'm asked what I'm thinking my mind is simply vacant and so my reply is made with a clear, vacant conscience.

I'm approaching a precipice. Each day I'm drawn nearer to the edge. I look only at the view. I avoid looking at the drop but I know what's there. At least, I can imagine it. I don't want to be asked either question, the conversation must be kept moving, hopping across the surface of our lives like a smooth flat stone.

Thought is not the point. I am feeling it, the flush, the rush of blood, the sensation of, yes, swooning. It comes in waves. Does it show? I'm sure it must show on my face the way pain might, the way pain would show on my husband's face . . .

– Do you still love me? What are you thinking?

Tonight I couldn't even manage my usual 'Nothing'. It wouldn't come out right. I try it out in my head, practise it, imagine the word as it would come out. It would sound unnatural, false, a strangled, evasive mumble or else a spat denial. Either way it wouldn't pass. It would lead to probing. A strained, suspicious little duet would begin in the midst of preparing the dinner and I know where this edgy, halting tune leads, I know the notes by heart.

(Practice makes perfect. Up and down the same old scales until you can do them without tripping up, twisting fingers or breaking resolutions, without swearing, yelling, failing or resentment at the necessity of repetition. Without scales the fingers are insufficiently developed to be capable of . . . Until you can do it in your sleep, until you *do* do it in your sleep, up and down as fast as dexterity permits. Without practice, life skills also atrophy*.)

For years we've shared everything we had to share, which wasn't much at first and now is way too much. In the way of possessions at least. We started simply: one room, a bed we nailed together from pine planks and lasted a decade; a few lingering relics from previous couplings (and still I long to ditch that nasty little bronze figurine made by the woman before me. A troll face, with gouged-out eyes; scary at night, glowering from a corner of the bedroom). Money was scarce but new love has no need of money. Somewhere to go, to be together is all and we were lucky. We had that. Hell is love with no place to go.

While around us couples were splitting at the seams, we remained intact. In the midst of break-ups and break-outs, we tootled on, sympathetic listeners, providers of impromptu pasta, a pull-out bed for the night, the occasional alibi. We listened to the personal disasters of our friends but wondered, in private, in bed, alone together at the end of another too-late night, what all the fuss was about. Beyond our ken, all that heartbreak, all that angst. What did it have to do with us, our lives, our kids? We had no room for it. Nor, for that matter, a great deal of space for passion.

An example to us all, we've been told. You two are an example to us all. Of course it was meant to be taken with a pinch of salt, a knowing smile, but it was said frequently enough for the phrase to stick, as if our friends in their cracked, snapped, torn-to-shreds state, our friends who had just said goodbye to someone they loved, or someone they didn't love after all or any more, as if all of them were suddenly united in a wilderness of unrequited love. While we, in our dusty, cluttered

---

*atrophy: wither away

home had achieved something other than an accumulation of consecutive time together.

This is true, of course, and we can be relied upon to provide some display of the example that we are. My husband is likely to take advantage of the opportunity and engage in a bit of public necking. Me, I sling mud, with affection. Either way, between us we manage to steer the chat away from our domestic compatibility, top up our friends' drinks, turn up the volume on the stereo, stir up a bit of jollity until it's time to be left alone together again with our example. Our differences remain.

– Do you still love me? What are you thinking?

Saturday night. The children are asleep. Three little dark heads are thrown back on pillows printed with characters from Lewis Carroll, Disney and Masters of the Universe. Three little mouths blow snores into the intimate bedroom air. Upstairs, the neighbours' hammer tacks into a carpet, their dogs romp and bark, their antique plumbing gurgles down the wall but the children sleep on, their sweet breath rising and falling in unison.

We are able to eat in peace, take time to taste the food which my husband has gone to impressive lengths to prepare. The dinner turns out to be an unqualified success: the curry is smooth, spicy, aromatic, the rice dry, each grain distinct, each firm little ellipse brushing against the tongue. The dinner is a joy and a relief. My husband is touchy about his cooking and requires almost as much in the way of reassurance and compliments in this as he does about whether I still love him or not. A bad meal dampens the spirits, is distressing both to the cook and the cooked-for. A bad meal can be passed over, unmentioned but not ignored. The stomach, too, longs for more than simply to be filled. A bad meal can be worse than no meal at all.

But it was an excellent meal and I was wholehearted and voluble in my appreciation. Everything was going well. We drank more wine, turned off the overhead light, lit a candle, fetched the cassette recorder from the kids' room and put on some old favourites: smoochy, lyrical, emotive stuff, tunes we knew so well we didn't have to listen, just let them fill the gaps in our conversation. So far so good.

Saturdays have to be good. It's pretty much all we have. Of us, the two of us just. One night a week, tiptoeing through the hall so as not to disturb the kids, lingering in the kitchen because it's further away from their bedroom than the living-room, we can speak more freely, don't need to keep the talk turned down to a whisper. We drink wine and catch up. It is necessary to catch up, to keep track of each other.

Across the country, while all the little loved ones are asleep, wives and husbands, single parents and surrogates are sitting down together or alone, working out what has to be done. There are always things to be done, to make tomorrow pass smoothly, to make tomorrow work. I look though the glasses and bottles and the shivering candle flame at my husband. The sleeves of his favourite shirt – washed-out blue with pearly buttons, last year's Christmas present from me – are rolled up. His elbows rest on the table which he recently sanded and polished by hand. It took forever. We camped out in the living-room while coat after coat of asphyxiating varnish was applied. It looks good now, better than before. But was the effort worth the effect?

My husband's fine pale fingers are pushed deep into his hair. I look past him out of the kitchen window, up the dark sloping street at parked cars and sodium lights, lit windows and smoking chimneys, the blinking red eye of a plane crossing a small trough of blue-black sky. My house is where my life happens. In it there is love, work, a roof, a floor, solidity, houseplants, toys, pots and pans, achievements and failures, inspirations and mistakes, recipes and instruction booklets, guarantees and spare parts, plans, dreams, memories. And there was no need, nothing here pushing me. It is nobody's fault.

I go to play-parks a lot, for air, for less mess in the house, and of course because the kids like to get out. Pushing a swing, watching a little one arcing away and rushing back to your hands, it's natural to talk to another parent. It passes the time. You don't get so bored pushing, the child is lulled and amenable. There's no way of reckoning up fault or blame or responsibility, nothing is stable enough, specific enough to be held to account and that's not the point. The swing swung back, I tossed my hair out of my eyes and glanced up at a complete stranger, a father. The father smiled back.

We know each other's names, the names of children and spouses. That's about all. We ask few questions. No need for questions. We meet and push our children on swings and sometimes we stand just close enough for our shoulders to touch, just close enough to feel that fluttering hollowness, like hunger. We visit the park – even in the rain, to watch the wind shaking the trees and tossing cherry blossoms on to the grass, the joggers and dog-walkers lapping the flat green park – to be near each other.

Millions have stood on this very same ledge, in the privacy of their own homes, the unweeded gardens of their minds. Millions have stood on the edge, and tested their balance, their common sense, strength of will, they have reckoned up the cost, in mess and misery, have wondered whether below the netless drop a large tree with spread branches awaits to cushion their fall. So simple, so easy. All I have to do is rock on my heels, rock just a shade too far and we will all fall down. Two husbands, two wives and all the little loved ones.

Childhood

Fearless

Janice Galloway

There would be days when you didn't see him and then days when you did. He just appeared suddenly, shouting threats up the main street, then went away again. You didn't question it. Nobody said anything to Fearless. You just averted your eyes when he was there and laughed about him when he wasn't. Behind his back. It was what you did.

Fearless was a very wee man in a greasy gaberdine coat meant for a much bigger specimen altogether. Grey-green sleeves dripped over permanent fists so just a row of yellow knuckles, like stained teeth, showed below the cuffs. One of these fisted hands carried a black, waxed canvas bag with an inept burst up one seam. He had a gammy leg as well, so every second step the bag clinked, a noise like a rusty tap, regular as a heartbeat. He wore a deceptively cheery bunnet like Paw Broon's over an escape of raw, red neck that hinted a crewcut underneath; but that would've meant he went to the barber's on a regular basis, keeping his hair so short, and sat in like everybody else waiting his turn, so it was hard to credit, and since you never saw him without the bunnet you never knew for sure. And he had these terrible specs. Thick as the bottoms of milk bottles, one lens patched with elastoplast. Sometimes his eyes looked crossed through these terrible specs but it was hard to be sure because you didn't get to look long enough to see. Fearless wouldn't let you.

There was a general assumption he was a tramp. A lot of people called him a tramp because he always wore the same clothes and he was filthy but he wasn't a tramp. He had his own house down the shorefront scheme; big black finger-stains round the keyhole and the curtains always shut. You could see him sometimes, scrabbling at the door to get in, looking suspiciously over his shoulder while he was forcing the key to fit. There were usually dirty plates on the doorstep too. The old woman next door cooked his meals and laid them on the step because he wouldn't answer the door. He sometimes took them and he sometimes didn't. Depended on his mood. Either way, there were usually dirty plates. The council cut his grass, he had daffodils for christsake – he wasn't a tramp. He was the kind that got tramps a bad name: dirty, foul-mouthed, violent and drunk. He was an alkie all right, but not a tramp: the two don't necessarily follow.

The thing about Fearless was that he lived in a state of permanent anger. And the thing he was angriest about was being looked at. Sometimes he called it MAKING A FOOL OF and nobody was allowed to get away with it. It was a rule and he had to spend a lot of time making sure everybody knew it. He would storm up and down the main street, threatening, checking every face just in case they were looking then if he thought he'd caught you he would stop, stiffen and shout WHO ARE YOU TRYING TO MAKE A FOOL OF and attack. Sometimes he just attacked: depended on his mood. Your part was to work out what sort of mood it was and try and adjust to it, make the allowance. It was what you were supposed to do. Most folk obliged, too – went out of their way to avoid his maybe-squinty eyes or pointedly NOT LOOK when they heard the clink and drag, clink and drag, like Marley's ghost, coming up the street. Then the air would fall ominously silent while he stopped, checking out a suspicious back, reinforcing his law. On a bad day, he would just attack anyway to be on the safe side. Just in case. You couldn't afford to get too secure. There was even a story about a mongrel stray he'd wound into a half-nelson because it didn't drop its gaze quick enough, but that was probably just a story. Funnier than the catalogue of petty scraps, blows that sometimes connected and sometimes didn't that made up the truth. It might have been true right enough but that wasn't the point. The point was you were supposed to laugh. You were meant to think he was funny. Fearless: the very name raised smiles and humorous expectations. Women shouted their weans in at night with HERE'S FEARLESS COMING, or squashed tantrums with the warning YOU'LL END UP LIKE FEARLESS. Weans made caricatures with hunchback shoulders, cross-eyes and a limp. Like Richard the Third. A bogeyman. And men? I have to be careful here. I belonged to the world of women and children on two counts, so I never had access to their private thoughts voiced in private places: the bookie's, the barber's, the pub. Maybe they said things in there I can have no conception of. Some may have thought he was a poor old soul who had gone to the bad after his wife left him. Romantics. I suppose there were some who could afford to be. Or maybe they saw him as an embarrassment, a misfit, a joke. I don't know. What I do know is that I never saw any of them shut him up when the anger started or try and calm it down. I remember what women did: leaving food on the doorstep and bottles for him to get money on; I remember women shaking their heads as he went past and keeping their eyes and their children low. But I don't remember any men doing anything much at all. He didn't seem to touch their lives in the same way. They let him get on with what he did as his business. There was a kind of respect for what he was, almost as though he had a right to hurl his fists, spit, eff and blind – christ, some people seemed to admire this drunken wee tragedy as a local hero. They called him *a character. Fearless is a character right enough* they would say and smile, a smile that accounted for boys being boys or something like that. Even polismen did it. And women who wanted to be thought above the herd – one of the boys. After all, you had to remember his wife left him. It was our fault really. So we had to put up with it the way we put up with everything else that didn't make sense or wasn't fair; the hard, volatile maleness of the whole West Coast Legend. You felt it would have been shameful, disloyal even, to admit you hated and feared it. So you kept quiet and turned your eyes away.

It's hard to find the words for this even now. I certainly had none then, when I was wee and Fearless was still alive and rampaging. I would keek out at him from behind my mother's coat, watching him limp and clink up the main street and not understand. He made me sick with fear and anger. I didn't understand why he was let fill the street with himself and his swearing. I didn't understand why people ignored him. Till one day the back he chose to stop and stare at was my mother's.

We were standing facing a shop window, her hand in mine, thick through two layers of winter gloves. The shop window was full of fireplaces. And Fearless was coming up the street. I could see him from the other end of the street, closer and closer, clinking the black bag and wheeling at irregular intervals seeing if he could catch somebody looking. The shouting was getting louder while we stood, looking in at these fireplaces. It's unlikely she was actually interested in fireplaces: she was just doing what she was supposed to do in the hope he'd leave us alone – and teaching me to do the same. Fearless got closer. Then I saw his reflection in the glass: three days' growth, the bunnet, the taped-up specs. He had jerked round, right behind where we were standing and stopped. He looked at our backs for a long time, face contorted with indecision. What on earth did he think we were plotting, a woman and a wean in a pixie hat? What was it that threatened? But something did and he stared and stared, making us bide his time. I was hot and cold at once, suddenly sick because I knew it was our turn, our day for Fearless. I closed my eyes. And it started. A lot of loud, jaggy words came out the black hole of his mouth. I didn't know the meanings but I felt their pressure. I knew they were bad. And I knew they were aimed at my mother. I turned slowly and looked: a reflex of outrage beyond my control. I was staring at him with my face blazing and I couldn't stop. Then I saw he was staring back with these pebble-glass eyes. The words had stopped. And I realised I was looking at Fearless.

There was a long second of panic, then something else did the thinking for me. All I saw was a flash of white sock with my foot attached, swinging out and battering into his shin. It must have hurt me more than it hurt him but I'm not all that clear on the details. The whole thing did not finish as heroically as I'd have liked. I remember Fearless limping away, clutching the ankle with his free hand and shouting about a liberty, and my mother shaking the living daylights out of me, a furious telling off, and a warning I'd be found dead strangled up a close one day and never to do anything like that again.

It was all a long time ago. My mother is dead, and so, surely, is Fearless. But I still hear something like him; the chink and drag from the close-mouth in the dark, coming across open, derelict spaces at night, blustering at bus stops where I have to wait alone. With every other woman, though we're still slow to admit it, I hear it, still trying to lay down the rules. It's more insistent now because we're less ready to comply, look away and know our place. And I still see men smiling and ignoring it because they don't give a damn. They don't need to. It's not their battle. But it was ours and it still is. I hear my mother too and the warning is never far away. But I never could take a telling.

The outrage is still strong, and I kick like a mule.

Feathered Choristers

Brian McCabe

Hello. I'm outside the door again, I can talk to you. You're not like anybody else in the class. You're from Mars, you're a Martian. That's why I can talk to you, because I'm not like anybody else in the class either. Sometimes you sit beside me don't you, when you want to ask me a question. Like what is one take away one on Earth. And I tell you the answer, nothing. Or when you want to tell me an answer, you materialise like in *Star Trek*. Just for a thousandth billionth of a second, then vanish back to Mars. Nobody sees you except me, nobody wants to. Nobody knows how to see you except me. See the dust in the air up there, where the sun's coming through the window? You're like the dust in the air – nobody notices you except me. And your voice is like interference on the radio – nobody wants to hear it except me. *You* can see everything. You can see through people, and you can see through walls. You've got X-ray eyes, that's why. I wish I had X-ray eyes. Cheerio.

Hello, come in, are you receiving me? My situation is an emergency, I have lost all contact with the *Enterprise*. I've been put outside the door again, because of my abominable behaviour. I am on the brink of disaster, and the teacher says my behaviour is deterior-hating. It means getting worse. This is an SOS. I will continue until I am rescued or until my Oxygen runs out. I'll tell you what's been happening to me down here on the planet Earth. Last week she made me sit next to the Brains. The Brains is an Earthling, species girl. With red hair, freckles and specs. I had to sit next to the Brains. She was always too hot, always wheezing and sweating, and her legs were always sticking to the seat. It was the noise I hated, the noise her legs made when she unstuck them from the seat. And she wouldn't let me use her red pencil, to colour in the sea. I know the sea's supposed to be blue on *Earth*, but on Mars it's red isn't it? And when I took that red pencil of hers out of her hand and broke it, the Brains started crying. It wasn't real crying, it was a special Earthling kind of crying. Sometime they cry outside but not inside, it's more like watering eyes. And in the middle of the crying she said something about my clothes, because I've got a patch on the back of my trousers. I can't see it, but everybody else in the class can. So I got her back in the playground. I went into the Earthling boys' toilets and I drew up some of the water, the pisswater in the pan, into my new fountain pen. Then I squirted it into her face, and it went all over her specs. And that's how I got into trouble last week, all because I got a new fountain pen. I don't like using these Earthling fountain pens much, they make too much of a fucking mess. Yesterday the teacher held my writing up for everybody in the class to look at, so they wouldn't write like me. See I don't write like anybody else, see I write in a kind of Martian. Nobody can read it except me and you, it's in code that's why. See all the mistakes are secret for something, every blot is a secret wee message. But I got into the worse kind of trouble for squirting piss into the Brains' face. The Mad Ringmaster got me, watch out for the Mad Ringmaster. Over and out, cheerio.

Hello, come in Mars, do you read me? My position is getting more abominable by the minute. So now she makes me sit on my own, so you can sit in the seat next to me. But you shouldn't materialise like that in the class, when everybody's listening to the radio. Everybody was listening to Rhyme Time, a programme of verse for Earthling children. Everybody thought it was interference, but I knew it was your voice talking to me. And I got put outside the door again because of you. Don't try and deny it, I did. It was that poem called Spring, all about the cuckoo and whatnot. And you were asking me what that poem was all about, because there aren't any birds on Mars, are there? And I saw you out of the corner of my eye, except you kept disappearing and coming back. Materialising. When I throw a stone in a puddle, everything disappears and comes back. That's what you're like, a reflection. So I had to tell you what Spring is and what a cuckoo is, so I started making the noise a cuckoo makes. *Kookoo, kookoo* – it sounds like its name. She thought I was taking the piss out of the programme, but I wasn't. I was talking to you in the secret wee voice, the one I'm talking in now. Billy Hope, she said, this is a classroom not a home for mental defectors. Go and stand outside the door, come back when the poetry programme's finished. But it isn't finished, because when I put my ear on the door I can hear it going on. She said it was bad enough having to put up with interference on the radio, without having to toler-hate interference from me.

I can't stand poetry anyway, it's worse than long division.

Maybe the next time you materialise, I'll use some sign-language to talk to you. I could scratch my nose for Hello. Everybody would think I was just scratching my nose. But then, if I had an itchy nose and I scratched it, maybe you'd think I was saying Hello. And if I stuck my tongue out for Cheerio, I'd get put outside the door every time I said Cheerio to you because of my abominable behaviour. I just put my ear to the door again and I heard the interference. It was you asking me another question, asking me what behaviour means. The answer is, I don't know.

I'll tell you something though: my mother's got a screw loose, has yours?

Over and out cheerio.

Hello come in are you receiving me? Listen: You were born on the same day as I was, at exactly the same time, except *you* were born on Mars. You go to a primary school on Mars, and you're in 4B like me. You're last in the class on Mars, except it's great to be last on Mars. It's like being top of the class on Earth. And 4B is better than 4A there isn't it, because everything's a reflection the other way round. You're like me the other way round. If I looked at you too much, I'd go cross-eyed like the Brains. See when you materialise in the seat that's empty, the seat next to mine – that's you doing your homework, isn't it? It's like Nature Study, except you're doing it on us the Earthlings. I bet you're glad you're not at a school on Earth. With a voice that sounds like interference, you'd get put outside the door every day. I wish you'd take me to your Martian school with you. Then I'd be top of the class – I mean last – and then *I'd* be called the

Brains. We'd be first – I mean last – equal. In the Martian primary school we'd get put outside the door for coming top of the class, because that's what the prize is on Mars. On Earth it isn't a prize, nobody likes it down here. And when you're put outside the door on Mars, you can travel through space and time. You can visit other planets. Down here there's nothing to do outside the door, there's nothing to look at. Nothing except the door. And the corridor, and the clock. Earthling clocks tell the time, every tick means a second. A second, a second, a second. No it doesn't *say* it, it tells the time with its hands. No it doesn't really have *hands*, it's a machine. No it doesn't have a mind, Earthling machines don't have minds. But cuckoo clocks say the time, they say *koo-koo, koo-koo*. But birds are different from clocks. See the birds on the windowsill up there, I think they're pecking for crumbs. You should do some Nature Study on them, because there aren't any birds on Mars, are there?

Or maybe there are some birds on Mars, but they look more like cuckoo clocks. But the clocks on Mars fly round and chirp the time.

Anyway I'll tell you what to say about Earthling birds. Put down that they've got wings, beaks, claws, feathers, tails and they fly. They eat worms and crumbs, and sometimes they migrate. It means go to Africa. See when they peck for crumbs they look like they're bowing, like actors at the end of a pantomime. Maybe they're all going to migrate to Mars, so they're bowing to say cheerio. I don't know if birds've got minds, but they must have minds to tell each other it's time to migrate. But they don't look like they've got minds because they move about in wee jerks like clockwork. Clocks don't have minds. But birds fly, clocks don't. But aeroplanes and spaceships fly and they don't have any minds. Tell you what, put down that you don't know if birds've got minds or not, but put down that the Earthling people *do* have minds in their heads. Now I bet you're wondering what all this has to do with Nature Study. I bet you're saying to yourself, this sounds more like Martian poetry to me. But have you ever thought that the two subjects might be quite the very same? Especially when there's interference on the radio, the two subjects sort of blur with each other, don't they?

I'll tell you something else: my mother put her head in the gas oven and she lost her mind.

Cheerio.

Listen if you don't pay attention, you'll never learn anything. Materialise *this instant*. That's better. If I catch you disappearing again or tuning out, I'm just going to have to make an example of you. Is that clear? Or else I will put you outside the door of your capsule and you will die. You're not stupid, you're lazy. You're a lazy, little *Martian*. You have opened my eyes more than once today and your behaviour is getting deterior-hating. Right, we're going to do some more Martian Nature Study. Any more interference out of you and I will give you long division or even poetry. Put this down:

Nature Study On The Planet Earth.

Under that, put this:

On the Planet Earth, everything is the other way round. Most Earthling birds don't have names and their mothers forget what to call them when they go to visit the nest. The only ones with names are crows, thrushes, blackbirds, sparrows, eagles, vultures and cuckoos. The rest are just called birds. Cuckoos are off their heads, they lay their eggs in the gas oven. My mother can be heard on the first day of Spring, and the noise she makes sounds like her name. She is cuckoo so she lives in a home, her home in another bird's next. Behaviour means going to Africa, or else abominable long division. A bird is a flying machine, with a screw loose. Cuckoo clocks have minds, as well as hands, faces and speckled breasts. At dawn you can hear them tick, and every tick means deterior-hating. Spring is the time of the year when you scratch your nose for Hello and stick out your tongue for Cheerio. Poetry is people pecking for crumbs without minds in their heads. After a pantomime, the actors migrate. I am dust in the air, I am a reflection. I am the only Earthling with a mind, and the mind is interference from another programme. Koo-koo, koo-koo.

Cheerio.

Come in again, do you read me, hello. See that door along there, behind that there's a wee room where you go to get smallpox jags. On the wall there's this chart with letters on it. On the top line the letters are huge, you'd have to be blind not to read them. But they get tinier and tinier as they go down, till you can hardly even see them. See this chart is for testing Earthling eyes. If you don't get far enough down, you get specs. I got specs, but I smashed them on the way to school because everybody was calling me four-eyes.

Nobody's going to call me four-eyes.

The Brains wears specs, but nobody calls her four-eyes. Probably because she's always had specs, so nobody notices them. If you ask me, the Brains was probably *born* with specs on. And I had to get specs because of you. Don't try and deny it. It's with looking at you when you materialise, now my eyes are the wrong way round. I wish I had X-ray eyes, then I could see into all the classrooms, I could see what's happening inside them. The last time I was in that room, that room with the chart on the wall, I got drops in my eyes that made me see a bit like a Martian. People didn't have edges, they sort of merged with each other. Blurred. But once when I was taken into that room this nurse in a white coat gave me a book to look at. It was a Martian book. Every page was covered all over with hundreds of coloured dots. They looked like they were moving, sort of swarming like wasps. It was like what you see when you look at the sun too long, hundreds of coloured dots moving round. Then this nurse asked me if I could make out the shape or the number. Everybody in the class had to do it, it was a test. I'll tell you this, I was great at it. I was better than anybody else in 4B. If we got tests in making out the shape or the number instead of tests in long division, I'd be getting fucking gold stars every time.

The trouble is we didn't get marks for it. It was to find out if we were colourblind. I'm not colourblind, I *know* the sea's supposed to be blue. It isn't though is it, when you look at it up close? When my mother used to take me to the seaside, the sea always looked more sort of like the colour of piss. And what about the Black Sea, what colour's that? I should ask the teacher: please Miss, is the Black Sea black? Miss, is the Red Sea red? What colour's the Dead Sea, Miss? Is that the one he walked on, or is that the one he parted? Miss how could he part a *sea*? Keep the noise down, it was a miracle. A miracle is something that doesn't happen every day on Earth. On Mars, everything that happens is called a miracle.

She put her head in the Dead Sea. Her mind got walked on, and parted. Keep the noise down, it was a miracle, miracle, miracle.

Over and out.

Hello. See it might be okay getting put outside the door, except everybody sees the patch. That's the deterior thing about it. See everybody knows I've got a patch in the back of my trousers, but when I'm walking out to the door everybody sees it at once. And I can feel this evil thing behind me, like an actor in a pantomime. Maybe people are like birds and don't have minds in their heads, maybe I'm the only Earthling with a mind. Everything else is a pantomime: everything everybody says, everything everybody does. Maybe even the Mad Ringmaster hasn't got a mind. I don't know if he has got a mind, because I can't be him. I've got to be me. But I know I've got a mind, but everything else could be a sort of colourblind pantomime. Like the Brains crying outside but not inside when I broke her fucking coloured pencil and squirted the piss on her specs. And the way my mother used to cry when she was losing her mind. She still does when I go to see her, but it's just like watering eyes. The tears drip out of her eyes like when a tap needs a new washer. She lost her mind, that's why. When you lose your mind on Earth, you go into a home for mental defectors. I've still got a mind, so I'm not going to be going into a home.

Hello mind, take me to Mars.

On Mars, everybody has a mind and you can *see* it. It looks like a page in that colourblind book. You look at all the swarming dots, you don't know what it is, then you make out the shape or the number. And that's what they're thinking, that's the thought. On Earth, people have to use words. They have to talk to each other, or write letters to each other, or phone each other up. If you want to talk to a lot of people at once, you have to be a teacher. Either that or you have to be on the radio or the t.v. Then you can talk to hundreds of people at once. Like the weatherman who was on before the Rhyme Time programme, except there was a lot of interference. Well, he was probably talking to about a million people at once. That's what I'm going to be when I grow up, I'm going to be the weatherman.

Cheerio.

Hello come in are you receiving me. In a few minutes there will be Clock Talk, a programme of verse for cuckoos. Before that we have a weather report from Mars:

> *This is the Martian weather forecast. Tonight it is going to rain smallpox. The air will be full of interference, and the sea will be going on fire later on. Don't part it or walk on it, and don't go out without getting your jags. Tomorrow morning, the sun is going to be a shape or a number. If you can't make it out, you're colourblind. The clouds are going to start off huge and get tinier and tinier as they go down. If you can't read them, you'll get specs. There will be a lot of abominable behaviour later on, so don't get put outside the door. There will be no gold stars for anybody this week, or the next. Instead the sky is going to be covered in mistakes and blots. In the North, and South, and East, and West, there will be some scattered showers. You're bound to get drops in your eyes. The planet is changing shape. Watch out for meteors. Cheerio.*

But if other people don't have minds, there isn't much point in talking to them, is there? Not even to one of them. Maybe you should score out the bit about Earthling people having minds, and put down that some do and some don't. And she doesn't talk to anybody except herself. See she lost her mind, then went into a home, and now she's got *two minds*. And one mind talks to the other mind, I think. But I wonder if the other mind can hear it. Maybe it's more like interference. But what I can't understand is how one mind take away one mind equal two minds.

Over and out.

Hello this is an sos. My Oxygen supply is running low and I have made no contact with the *Enterprise*. Beam me up before it's too late.

See down there over that balcony, that's the Assembly Hall. It means prayers. You put your hands together and you say: *Our Father Which Art in Heaven, Hallo'ed Be Thy Name*. Then the Mad Ringmaster stands up and everybody else sits down and listens. He makes a speech about the school. If you've squirted piss on somebody's specs, he reads out your name and you have to report to his study along the corridor there. Or if something's happened in the school, the Mad Ringmaster announces it. Like when one boy died, he announced it so that everybody would know. He said: *Today there is a shadow among us*. He's like you that boy, dematerialised. Nobody can see him. See he fell from a tree, and the blood ran over his brain. His soul went to Heaven, and his mind is a shadow among us. On Mars you probably have a different kind of assembly. You probably just sit in a big circle holding hands, passing messages to each other through your fingertips. Because hundreds of Martians can get together and think *one* thought, because you can sort of merge, can't you? Blur with each other.

I wish I was an alien being. Maybe the next time you materialise, if you touch me we'll maybe merge.

So I had to report to his study. I told everybody about it in the playground, I was the centre of attention. Attention is what you pay for somebody talking to you. It's like buying something with money, you have to pay it to hear what they say. I told them all your name for him, the Mad Ringmaster, but everybody just said his name's Williams. You call him that because that's sort of what he looks like, with his big black gown and curly mustache. And his belt instead of a whip. And I told everybody what he said to me in his study, when he was giving me the belt. You'd better start crying. See, he wanted me to cry on the outside, the way the Brains did, the way my mother does. Like an actor in a pantomime. Then he could make an example of me. He could take me back to the class crying and then I'd be an example.

I am an example. But what am I an example of? I'm an example of *you*, the other way round. I should tell the teacher: Please Miss, I'm the wrong way round. Billy Hope, this is a classroom not a home for mental defectors. Go and stand outside the door. You can come back in when you're the right way round.

But if the Mad Ringmaster ever gets me again, I'm definitely going to go to Mars. He'll have to announce it at assembly: *There is a shadow . . . no not a shadow . . . there is a reflection among us. He got put outside the door, and the blood ran over his brain*. I wish you would exterminate the Mad Ringmaster, make *him* a shadow among us. Put him in a box and bury him, bury him in the Dead Sea. It's wrong to hope somebody dies, except on Mars. What's wrong here on Earth is right on Mars, or at least it's not wrong. Because not wrong isn't the same as right always is it? Like when you get a test, and you don't know some of the answers. So you don't put anything down, you just leave them blank. Well, you're not wrong, are you? But you're not right either, or they'd give you marks. They'd give you a couple of marks for leaving it blank, but they don't, except on Mars.

You know something, if they gave her a test she wouldn't be able to answer any of the questions. She'd get nothing out of a hundred. *Here comes the Mad Ringmaster*.

I'm inside the class again, I can't talk to you. He got me again, for getting put outside the door. He wanted me to cry on the outside again, to make me an example. But I didn't, I cried inside. My hands are on fire, they're Martian hands. Touch my fingertips, touch. Send messages through my fire. Don't ask me any more questions, blur with me. My hands are full of a thousand stings, so are yours. It feels like a swarm of wasps, a thousand stings. You can feel the message, so can I. It's sore that's the message. The teacher's reading that poem called Spring from a book. Pay attention, pay attention. Cheerio.

'Billy Hope, stop blowing on your hands. I'm going to read the first verse again, the one you missed because of interference.

Perhaps you can tell us what it means, Billy. Listen to the words very carefully:

Pretty creatures which people the sky
Are thousandfold this day,
Feathered choristers, they that sing
The livelong day away.

Now, Billy, I want you . . .'

I am an alien being and I people the thousandfold sky.

'I want *you* to tell the class . . . what the feathered choristers are.'

My Mother put her head in the sky and her mind flew away.

'Birds.'

Striker

(fur Neal Pryce)

Matthew Fitt

Luke's twelfth grade Historical Biology teacher, Mr Seltzer, wis in slaver over-drive. His heid filled the screen in the corner o Luke's bedroom afore it wis replaced by a pictur o a green beastie. 'This is a visual of the South American tree frog,' havered Mr Seltzer, 'which was made extinct in the year 2035. Check out its colouring and shape. What does it remind you of? Enter a thought in your lapbooks now.'

Luke thocht the South American puddock* looked like Mr Seltzer's pus but he didnae enter *that* intae his lapbook. He didnae dare. Mr Seltzer wisnae extinct, altho he wis in Chicago. Chicago wis thoosans o kms awa fae Dumfries but if Seltzer got cheek fae ony o his on-line cless o twelfth graders spreid aroon the warld, he'd tak a foamy. He'd mibbe dae whit he did tae puir Rui Roshinhio fae Brazil.

Rui pit thegither a repro model o a lang deid member o the ape faimlie cryed an Orangutang an stuck a graphic o the Historical Biology teacher's heid on tap o the monkey's boady, syne e-mailed it tae aw his clessmates' screens roon the planet. When ane ended up by mistake in Seltzer's doocot at the WestSchool main office in Chicago, Auld Seltzy went radgie* supernova. He poued the plug on Rui's WestSchool link-up in Brazil an consequently on wee Rui's future wi WestCo. If Luke ever did onythin tae guddle up* his ain future wi WestCo, Luke's faither wid kill him.

Luke tholed* the lesson aboot puddocks that yaised tae lowp aboot in Sooth America tae the end. Altho he aye cawed

---

*puddock: frog
*radgie: crazy
*guddle up: mess up
*tholed: put up with

canny* aroon Mr Seltzer, he switched aff the screen afore he'd heard his hamework. He couldnae help hissel. It didnae maitter if the WestSchool attendance computer registered him slippin awa early or no. He could aye blame it on a pouer-cut an if the hamework exercise wis a sair yin, his baw-heid neebor, Massimo in Italy, wid soon enough e-mail him up fur the answers an he could git the hamework aff him. Luke couldna gie a fleein giga-byte if the schule kent or no. It wis Seturday. Glesga were at hame tae Madrid. An naethin else on the planet maittered.

He'd been up tae hi-doh aw moarnan, chappin the leg o his chair wi his guttie, enterin glaikit answers tae simple questions, his mind hotchin wi crosses, penalties an goals insteid o makkin notes aboot barkit* bauchled* wee beasties. Luke thocht maist o thaim were that boaky-lookin it wis a guid joab they were deid onywey. Luke didna care aboot onythin but Glesga an Madrid. He pit oot auld Seltzy's puddock-like geggie* pronto an cleared his desk. He had better things tae dae. He wis gaun roon tae Flynn's fur tae watch the big gemm on Flynn's new CyberStation.

Luke's ma wis doon the stair goin the messages in the front room. She looked like she wis daein some kind o auld-farrant* war dance or the mating ritual o the extinct euro-asian peacock he'd been learnin aboot the ither day. He chapped the 'pause' button on the faimlie's scartit* auld oot-dated HelpMaster system that aye gied Luke a riddie every time ony o his pals come in the hoose an seen it. His ma stapped hauf-wey doon the Syntho-veggie section an momentarily left the Virtual Supermarket environment tae hear fae her son.

'Hurry, Luke,' she sayd, in that mealie-moothed NewCal English wey she had that made Luke's stomach lowp* like a garbage mixer. 'There's a special on frozen whale this week-end

---

*cawed canny: exercised caution
*barkit: dirty
*bauchled: useless
*geggie: face
*auld-farrant: old-fashioned
*scartit: scratched
*lowp: jump

and you know how tense your father gets if he hears he's missed out on some gourmet beluga.'

Luke wis sair tempted tae hit the 'play' button an let his ma pauchle* on doon the supermerkit dreel tae the great muckle gless bunkers o synthetic sea meat. Fur a stert, she wis aboot as bauchled as the muckle great HelpMaster unit, no juist her claes or her hair, but the wey she stood. The wey she wis. Secondly tho, the thocht o her beatin aw the ither wifies an hoose husbands tae the stots o whale meat an so guaranteein an oor or twa wi his faither bein no sae radge as usual wis a muckle incentive tae. His faither had taen the stress shuttle tae Holland fur the efterninn fur a roond o buddy gowf wi his WestCo workmates as pairt o the company's rage management program. He widna be back til late.

Luke didna hurl his mither back intae shoppin limbo. 'I'm away to Dermot Flynn's,' he sayd, shauchlin* taewards the door. 'I'll be back at eighteen.'

'Not a minute later,' his ma replied. 'I'm re-microing yesterday's stork burgers and if you're good, your father may share some beluga with you.'

Luke wis near oot the door.

'Do you have enough euros on your card?' she spiered* him. Luke's credit panel wis usually fou o spankies* the nou.

'Ay,' he flung back intae the room an turned tae leave.

'Luke!' He heard his mither's kenspeckle* lug-nippin high-pitched skraik* an turned back. 'That is not how we speak in this house and certainly not what you learn at WestSchool. I will ask you again. Do you have enough money?'

'Yes, mother,' Luke replied wi a heavy mooth. His mither didnae like him speakin Auld. 'I'll be home at six, mother.' A crouse*

---

*pauchle: shuffle
*stots: lumps
*shauchlin: slouching
*spiered: asked
*spankies: new money
*kenspeckle: well-known
*skraik: screech
*crouse: arrogant

wee victory smile spreid across her triple x foondation cream beclartit* cheeks like a crack openin up in Earthquake America an Luke pushed 'play'. She kerried on mimin her wey down the supermerkit aisle. Luke quit the hoose.

Flynn steyed in ane o the big hooses up the brae. Flynn's faither had an auld ermy telescope an when they were bairns, Luke an Flynn had spent oors in the tap room o the hoose glowerin across the Irish Sea an keekin richt intae shop windaes in the hert o Belfast. Whiles they had been able tae mak oot the clouds o reek an smog that hingit owre the twin-city conurb o Manchester an Liverpool. But there were nane o thaim bairns ony mair. They were stieve* strappin junior adults nou. Luke an Flynn had ither things tae play at.

The brae tae Flynn's hoose wis a sair pech* an Luke trauchled* up it on the flittin* sidewalk. He hirpled* throug the avenue o birk* trees that led up tae Flynn's hoose an rang the bell. A security pad flipped oot at him as he stood hechin* at the front door. He registered his haun-prent wi the hoose computer an chapped his fowre-letter password intil the keyboard. The door opened an Flynn wis on the ither side.

'Hey, dude,' Flynn sayd, hucklin* a haunfou o blond hair awa fae his fore heid. 'Gemm's stertin. Hurry ben.' Luke follaed him throu the lang white ivory-tile lobby he yaised tae imagine wis the stert o the road tae heaven, an doon intae the basement o the muckle five-story hoose. Flynn's liquid disc music center wis skelpin oot Track 8 fae Gooseberry's new dog vid 'The Dress is Easy'. The Hammerslam drum beat stottit* roon the reid brick

---

*beclartit: smeared
*stieve: strong
*sair pech: hard climb
*trauchled: dawdled
*flittin: moving
*hirpled: limped
*birk: birch
*hechin: panting
*hucklin: folding
*stottit: bounced

basement space. Luke could feel his bluid stert tae gowp* in his veins. He wis chokin tae see Flynn's new Station. If it wis hauf as intense as Flynn had described it til him owre the face-phone, then this wis really gonnae be somethin tae wet his punders fur.

The Station wis skelp-new*. It sat on its lane at the faur end o the basement. Luke could mak oot twa muckle reid memory kists* as braid an as big as coffins. They were jined in the middle by a siller* cube. Luke kent thon wis the reality engine. Thon wis where the magic happened. 'Where's the suit, Flynn? How do I put it on?' Luke couldnae dam the torrent o havers* skitterin* oot his mouth.

'Yo, radge person. Tak a chill pill. Chow a caw-canny-granny-sooker, eh, an haud yir wheesht twa seconds. Captain Wilson Flynnsky is here and will give what you need.' Flynn wis ettlin* tae be cool but Luke kent his doh wis as high as his. Flynn hadnae been virtual witness at a live gemm yet. The haill thing wis new tae thaim baith. The blethers soon come skooshin oot o Flynn tae. As he poued Luke by the airm owre til the equipment, he stertit haverin aboot his da.

Flynn's faither worked fur MedCal Worldwide. He wis a surgeon. Fifteen meenits afore Flynn wis alloued tae git his clatty* wee hauns on the new equipment, faither Flynn, fae the basement o his hoose in Dumfries, had been up tae his oxters* in a hert-bypass op on a patient papped oot on a theatre bed ten thoosan kms awa in Singapore's Windsor Memorial Hospital, slicin throu veins an arteries wi a remote virtual scalpel. Luke didnae care. He wis cauld* tae talk o Flynn's

---

*gowp: run
*skelp-new: brand-new
*kists: chests
*siller: silver
*havers: nonsense
*skitterin: pouring
*ettlin: trying
*clatty: dirty
*oxters: armpits
*cauld: reluctant

faither. He micht hae been cuttin a daud o biled ham fur his denner. Luke wisnae intressit. This Station had the SportsInYourFace channel that naebody this side o Moscow could git an Luke waantit in.

Flynn redd up* Luke wi the richt gear. He made Luke pit on an electronic semmit. Juist as he wis gittin yaised tae the slidderie feel o the vest on his skin, Flynn slaistered a haunfou o conductor gel roon the side o Luke's heid. 'Oyah,' gret Luke. The jeely wis cauld. 'That's right, ma wee keekie-mammy,' sayd Flynn, dichtin his ain napper wi the gel. 'Just like in the Holywood CD-ROMS when the bad guy gets the chair.' Flynn skirled owre tae a postal kist wi the delivery-hap still on an returned wi twa VR helmets. Luke pit his on but left the bleck gless vizor up. Flynn did the same syne* went back tae the kist. He kerried owre twa gowden boxes. Luke rived* the box open. Inside wis a pair o gowden buits, glintin, keekin in the hauf licht o the room. He pit thaim on. The buits wis as licht as air.

'A minute to three. You ready?' sayd Flynn.
'Yes,' replied Luke an mindin his mither, added, 'Ay.'

Flynn chapped the word 'ready' intae the command panel. Luke felt a skitter o energy ripple throu the electrodes attached tae his heid. His wame* rummled* wi excitement. A lump the size o ane o his faither's Slazengers stuck in his thrapple*. Flynn hut the 'play' button an the reality engine came tae life wi an electronic pech. Luke an Flynn snapped thair vizors doon.

Bleckness.
A buzzin in the lug.

Pain stobbin doon the left side o the boady. A mind-shooglin sense o wechtlessness an the urgent need tae boak. Mair

---

*redd up: fixed up
*syne: then
*rived: tore
*wame: belly
*rummled: rumbled
*thrapple: throat

bleckness. Ainlie bleckness. A pitmirk* prospect unrelieved by ony licht. An the stomach, the geggie, the boak-bag gaun roon like a car wheel.

Fur a second, Luke waantit it stapped. This virtual world wisnae richt. It didnae feel guid. He waantit tae gang back tae reality. He waantit Flynn fur tae turn it aw aff, shaw him tae the nearest restroom, funn a shunkie an pit his heid doon it. But sic sairness soon passed. The mirk curtain poued back an Luke wis deeved* by the slotter o buits on concrete. A voice kittled* in his lug. FRAGOLA, ROJAS, HAMMER, BOROVSKY . . . a licht appeared up aheid o him, the clatter o studs cawin him forrit . . . WOLF, LE MAN, VAN HALEN. Luke bielded* his een. A bleeze brichter nor the sun stumoured* him. A rummle-tummle orchestra o voices drooned the ane in his lug an drookit aw his senses. He felt hissel run oot ontae the pitch. A firework skitit by him. Stieve airms swung bricht muckle multi-coloured flags throu the reekin air. Big men wi lang sleekit bleck hair stood in a raw on either side o him wi thair hauns ahint thair backs, Glesga in reid, Madrid in white. SOLDAT, LAURENTIS, VANINIO. The wee voice focht tae be heard owre the loud, rauchle* yins. AND GRAY. The match commentator feenished the team leet wi the ainlie Scottish player in the Glesga side an a rair riz roon the groond like a plump o thunner.

'Luke. Yo, Luke.' Luke heard his ain name cawed oot owre aw the din. 'Luke. Up here.' Next thing Luke kent he wis a hunner metres up hingin owre the stadium in mid air wi Flynn hingin alangside him. 'Hey, thought ye'd like that. I programmed you to come out with the teams.' Luke keeked doon. He could see the haill arena. The players had skailed fae the touch line an were spreidin owre the pitch tae skelp practice baws intae their ain goals. Luke had a fear o hichts but he wisnae tellin Flynn

---

*pitmirk: pitch black
*deeved: deafened
*kittled: tickled, stirred
*bielded: shielded
*stumoured: stunned
*rauchle: rough

that. 'Can we try the main stand?' he spiered, pointin doon at the seated area ahint the Glesga goal, hotchin wi a rammy o boadies. 'That's so lame,' replied Flynn. 'Pick a player. Let's do POV. I'll go Rojas. Who do you want?' Luke waled oot Gray an in a second he wis back doon at pitch level, seein awthin fae Gray's point o view.

The gemm stertit an Gray got the baw furst. Luke felt a thrill slidder throu him. Gray took the baw roon a Madrid player. The Spaniards were in white an Luke saw a white-sleeved elba jouk* towards Gray's face. Luke flenched, shuttin baith his een. He opened thaim again a second later. Gray aye had the baw an wis hechin an pechin at full speed doon the weeng. Gray keeked up an in thon hauf-second Luke experienced Gray's realisation that a pass wis on tae Rojas tae the left o him. Luke willed his man tae chap the baw owre the turf but afore he could pou back his foot, the white jersey o Zenga, the muckle-boukit Madrid sweeper, wis scuddin across his path. Luke felt a shairp pain in his ankle an Gray wis skitin neb-doon on the gress.

'Why didn't you pass, you loser?' Flynn's voice nipped him. 'I was clear through on goal.'

Luke gied his pal the deef lug. He wisna enjoyin this as muckle as the thocht he wid. This wis gittin owre real. Flynn's faither's reality engine could reproduce a haill stadium. It could mak him feel every scart an skelp a player took. If a player went doon wi a terrible clatter, the thing micht be able tae replicate a gammy leg or burst heid on him. Luke tried tae soond bored. 'Where else can we go with this?'

'Let's try the executive box,' suggestit Flynn. 'See if we can catch any of the players' girlfriends.' Luke's mooth went dry. He'd seen some o thir women on terrestial tv. Maist o thaim hirpled aboot on the catwalk in cutty sarks* an high heels. They were shiny like new aipples, thair lips reid an thair een bricht. Lookin at thaim gart Luke's legs turn tae jeely. He stuttered tae Flynn that thon wis a guid idea but when the pair rematerialised owre the directors' box, they funn thair road barred. The virtual

---

*jouk: jerk
*cutty sarks: short dresses

programmers had wired in a bleck-oot code forenent the executive suite tae bield the high heid-yins an thair bonnie freens fae clarty-mindit wee boys like Flynn an Luke. The twa lads wis scunnered. They could mak oot neither breist or hurdie. Aw they could jalouse* wis a stushie* o shaddas an bogles flittin ahint a fug o static an distortion.

'I want a goal,' announced Flynn. 'My chip says that a score from Glasgow is imminent.'

'Who's most likely to get it?' Flynn wis eident* nou tae hurl himself back intae the gemm tae mak up fur bein feert earlier an fur no gittin tae keek doon some model's blouse. 'I'm going to go POV again.'

'Cool the beans, kid.' Flynn spoke wi a crabbit edge til his voice. There wisnae usually mony goals scored in a ticht gemm like this an Flynn waantit tae be in the richt place at the richt time if onybody hut the back o the net. The statistics computer wis whusperin in his lug that Rojas wid likely score in the next twa-three meenits. 'The chip's tellin me Gray's about to put one away. You go POV on Gray for a while. I'll take – let me see now – och, I'll take Rojas.' Flynn wis a canny liar.

'Thanks,' replied Luke, excitement kittlin ben in his hert like a fire. Luke thocht himsel owre intae Gray's boady. He kent that the player had nae idea he wis there. A shoogle o unpleasant thochts skitit throu him as he imagined the same thing happenin tae him. He widnae like a stranger inhabitin his boady, even if it wis juist fur a gemm o fitba.

A dunt on the heid brocht him back fae his dwam*. Gray had juist heidered the baw doon tae Le Man an Le Man wis chasin aff tae the ither side o the park. Gray wis miles awa fae the goal. He wis huckled forby. Luke wis aware of the semm pain fae that roch* challenge earlier, stobbin awa doon in his ankle. Altho Luke had nae control owre Gray's movement, he could feel exactly whit the player felt. An Gray seemed tae be aboot tae

---

*jalouse: guess at
*stushie: commotion
*eident: keen
*dwam: dream
*roch: rough, rash

cowp owre fae exhaustion. He didnae hae the strenth tae tie his ain shuin never mind run the lenth o the pitch tae the penalty box. Luke wis vexed. This couldna be richt. Mibbe Flynn's statistics wis wrang. Gray widnae even score in the next oor. Luke's auld granny had mair chance o grabbin a goal than him.

Luke took in the furious action up aheid. Gray wis caucht in defence an wis pechin his wey back up the pitch. The gemm burled roon the pitch at haliket* speed. There aye seemed tae be a rammy o players in orbit roon the baw, flittin across the park like a twister. Luke watched as a wide player floated a great cross in fae the corner flag. Rojas lowped up owre the shooders o the Spanish defence an skelped the baw wi his heid strecht at the Madrid goal. The keeper couldnae git aff his wrang fit an soon the baw wis a flash o white wheechin past his feckless raxin fingirs. The haill stadium wheesht. Luke held his tae, realisin wi a shairp pou on his hert that Flynn had pauchled him o a goal. He boued his heid, his lugs soon ringin wi Flynn's snochterie voice.

'Damn,' it said. Luke keeked up. Rojas hadnae scored. Luke saw the baw stot back aff the crossbar. He lauched. Serves the spoilt wee eejit right, thocht Luke, but afore he could interface wi Flynn an tell him where tae stick his keechie machine, he funn himsel pechin an hoastin* fae sudden exertion. Gray, he jaloused, had stertit tae run.

The baw had skitit aff the crossbar at sic a pace, it had rebounded tae near the hauf-wey line. The Spanish defence had forgot aw aboot Gray an naebody wis near him when he picked the baw up. As he cairried the baw forrit on his feet, Luke could sense Gray mak his choice. Rojas wis aff-side, Le Man and Wolf baith marked oot the gemm. The ainlie road in wis Route Wan, strecht throu the middle. Luke felt Gray's hert chap louder at his chist. He experienced the player tak in a lang lung-fou o air. Awthin disappeared forby the road tae goal. Luke wis nae langer aware of the rummle o the fans, nor could he tell if the loud drummin in his lugs wis Gray's hertbeat or his.

---

*haliket: crazy
*hoastin: coughing

The next five seconds wis as fast as a slap in the ja. Gray skinned yin defender. The baw sklaffed* aff the legs o anither. Zenga, the muckle, reid-beardit sweeper, flung himsel at Gray but Gray kept the heid an jouked roon him. When the Spanish keeper come chairgin oot, Gray wis the lown centre o a gallus* storm. Sweat run aff his neb. His hair hingit doon owre yin ee. He keeked up. The keeper's hauns wis near gruppin the baw. Gray's rigbane* tensed. He brocht his fit doon shairp unner the baw an it spun up, lowped the keeper an drapped richt intae the yawnin mooth o the goal.

WILLIE GRAY PUTS GLASGOW AHEAD. A BEAUTIFUL PENALTY BOX LOB STUNS THE MADRID PLAYERS. THE AULD FIRM FAITHFUL GO WILD BEHIND US HERE IN THE COMMENTARY POD. Luke couldnae credit the noise aroon him. His brain literally stapped as a wave o pure soond, whipped up by the hot braith fae seeventy thoosand thrapples, rattled his banes an biled the bluid inside his veins. His hert soared skyward. He forgot aw aboot Gray an alloued himsel tae believe it wis him lowpin owre the advertisin boards takkin the accolades o the Glesga crowd. LUKE PATERSON, he heard as he flung his reid Glesga FC sark intae the main stand, HAS REALLY SET THIS GAME ALIGHT. LUKE PATERSON HAS SCORED AN INCREDIBLE GOAL. MADRID HAVE NO ANSWER TO THE MIGHTY LUKE PATERSON.

'Luke Paterson, ya wee bampot.' Luke could hear Flynn fizzin away in the background. 'That was my goal. You took my goal.' Luke didna care. He'd scored his goal. He kent nou whit it wis like tae mak thoosans o people chant yir name. 'Paterson, you're outa here, boy. I'm through with you.' Flynn's greetin voice didna maitter. Luke couldna hear it onywey. He wid git nae higher than this. It didnae come ony better than this.

Syne awthin went deid. Luke wis back in Flynn's faither's basement again. Flynn had cut him oot o the gemm. Luke liftit the vizor fae aff his face. Flynn wis staunin aside him, cairryin

---

*sklaffed: ricocheted
*gallus: outrageous
*rigbane: spine

on wi the match on his ain. Luke kent the script weel. His posh pal did this fae time tae time. It wis Flynn's baw an Luke wisnae gettin tae play. Luke poued aff aw the virtual witness gear an shawed himsel oot the hoose.

Tae mak the warm feelin ben in his hert last as lang as he could, Luke went hame by a road he didnae usually tak. It took him roon by the high flats an alang the side o the river.

A puckle o laddies wis blooterin a fitba tae each anither on a square o gress. They were aw guid. Luke wis surprised they werenae watchin the big gemm. As he hurried alang past thaim, he thocht o the sheer gallusness o Gray's wee chip owre the Spanish goalkeeper and re-run in his heid the radge celebrations o the Glesga F.C. fans. Luke wis in mid-dauner throu this dwam when somethin fremmit* hut aff his leg. It wis a baw.

'See's it back, eh?' Ane o the laddies cryed owre til him. Luke keeked up. He saw he wis near the twa jaikets set oot on the gress fur goals. He realised he wis in exactly the same position as he wis when Gray chipped Cabuta. He kent whit tae dae. He stepped up tae the baw, poued his left fit back an brocht his guttie doon hard on the grund. The baw spun up, wheeched throu the air at an unco angle, stottit aff the grund aboot twinty feet fae the goals an run awa doon intae the river. The laddies went daft. Ane skelped owre tae the river bank tae retrieve the baw. The lave* came breengin* up tae Luke wi thair een as haurd as nieves. Luke turned an tried tae hirple awa, his face as reid as Willie Gray's shirt. Luke's mooth went dry.

He had never kicked a baw in his life.

---

*fremmit: strange
*lave: the rest
*breengin: rushing

Rupert Bear and the San Izal

Alan Spence

I opened the Rupert Bear book and laid it flat on my lap. Not that I could read it. There were too many words, a dense block of print under each frame. But I followed the story in pictures, made my own sense of it.

The house was quiet, filled with the strangeness of being alone. My father was at work, my mother had gone out to the shops. I was not long up out of bed, had been sick, with a fever, for a week. That was why I wasn't at school.

I sat in the kitchen, keeping warm by the fire.

The Rupert book was one of three I had been given at Christmas. The others were the Beano Annual and a book of Bible stories. I had kept all three close by me this past week, read through them and through them again. The Beano book was the easiest. The words were simple, came out in balloons, straight from the characters' mouths. The Bible stories were too difficult, solid columns of narrative and only one picture to a page. I had busied myself by colouring some of the pictures with stubs of wax crayon. But the lines were a scrawl, were never neat enough, were all the wrong colours. In one picture I had given God an orange face and green hair, a black crown and a cloak made up of all the colours I had, one on top of another. And I couldn't contain the colours within the outlines. They streaked over onto other things in the picture – clouds, a bird, the sun. Frustrated, I had scored a heavy black line across the page and scribbled over the words that I couldn't read. That was why I had put the book from me and turned instead to Rupert Bear.

The Rupert stories were very mysterious. Rupert lived with his mother and father in a snug house, a thatched cottage with its own garden. But he was forever wandering off, sometimes on his own, sometimes with his friend Algy. He would discover a secret door or a hidden passage that led through to some enchanted place. There was a beautiful little Chinese girl called

Tiger Lily. Her father was a Conjurer and could make magic. He would set Rupert off on fantastic adventures. But no matter how far away he went, how strange the worlds he entered, he always found his way back. Home. Safe.

My mother had been gone a long time. I was hungry.

I climbed on a chair and ransacked the kitchen cabinet, but there was nothing. A bottle of sauce. Salt and pepper. A packet of rice. Nothing I could eat. Left in its greaseproof wrapper was the last slice of a pan loaf. The ender. Outsider. It was curled and beginning to go hard, but it didn't look too bad. There was a lump of margarine, solid from the cold and hard to cut and spread. But I managed to slice a bit off, scrape it and press in on to the bread. The whole mess was crumbly and uneven. I sprinkled sugar over it. A sugary piece. The bread was dry and tasted half-stale. I laid it down on the table after a bite or two, closed up the kitchen cabinet, put the knife I had been using into the sink.

The Rupert book was lying open, face-down where I had left it, and looking I noticed something I hadn't seen before. The front and back covers made up one long picture, carried on over the spine. Before, I had seen them as separate, now I could see it whole. It was a wide vista. Rupert was in the foreground, cresting a hill, overlooking a valley, a few of his friends coming up the slope behind him. Tiger Lily and the Conjurer were in the valley itself, walking towards a golden pagoda. The valley was a magic land, flowery and lush. Trees grew around the pagoda and along the banks of a stream. There were parrots among the trees, tiny lizards in the grass, a black dragon coiled on an outcrop of rock. And in the sky, throwing a weird light over everything, was a shining globe, a planet, bright yellow and green against the deep blue of the sky. The Conjurer's arm was outstretched, finger pointing at the globe. I felt like crying, for no reason.

I got up and went through to the room, to look out the window for my mother. From the room I could see our street and another leading off it down towards the docks. Rows of grey tenements, a factory, wasteground. There were only a few people. A huddle of men at the corner. A scatter of children on the wasteground, too young for school, or off sick like me. Women moving from close to shop and back again, but no mother. Through the thin walls I could hear a radio playing in the house next door. *Yellow bird, up high in banana tree . . .* I liked the song, but not the singer's voice. I went back through to the kitchen, feeling cold.

Mechanically, I picked up the bread I had left on the table and took another bite, chewed it to a dry pulp, sweet sugary grit between my teeth. I couldn't finish it, threw the last hard crust into the bucket.

The kitchen window looked out over the back court, the backs of the buildings, a grey square. My mother's washing, pegged on a line, hung limp. A dog snuffled in the midden, among the rubbish and the ash. Nothing else moved. There was nothing to see. In the sink lay the knife I had used, still streaked with margarine. I turned on the tap, let the rush of water splash over it, but it didn't come clean, was still smeared, the cold water clinging in globules to the blade.

Beside the sink was a dark green bottle of disinfectant. The name was in big red letters on the label. SAN IZAL. And in smaller letters, under a red cross, was the word POISON. That had been spelled out to me, with a warning to leave it alone. I unscrewed the cap and sniffed at the San Izal. I loved the strong smell of it, a smell you could just about bite. I wanted to take a sip, but it was poison. If I swallowed it I would die. My father said when you died that was it. Finished. There was nothing else. My mother said you went to Heaven to live with God. I thought of the God I had coloured in the Bible storybook, with his orange face and green hair. The strange feeling of sadness, of wanting to cry, was still on me, an emptiness inside. I put the cap back on the bottle, sat down again with my books.

I didn't try to read, just opened out the Rupert book, sat staring at the picture on the cover. I looked at every inch of it, saw every detail, every blade of grass, every figure. Rupert. Tiger Lily. The Conjurer, pointing. And again and again I was drawn to that globe in the sky, that perfect radiant sphere. The feeling was centred in my stomach and had something to do with the picture. I wanted my mother.

I held the book close to me and crossed once more to the sink. I wanted to drink the San Izal. The liquid was dark brown, treacly brown, but when you poured it into the sink it turned white. I tucked the book under my arm. I lifted the bottle and opened it. The dark smell from the green bottle. The circle of light in Rupert's sky. To be dead. To be finished. To be with God. To be nothing. The empty feeling inside. The lack. If I swallowed the poison I would know. I heard my mother's key turn in the door and she was here, she was home. The tears came now. I couldn't hold them back. I had put down the bottle and dropped the book on the floor. My mother dumped her message bag on the table, and 'Hey, what's the matter?' she said, laughing and hugging me. 'What's the matter?' And I wanted to tell her but I couldn't. I had no words.

Home

Saskatchewan

Lorn Macintyre

It's Games Day. The sun has risen over the bay and is coming through my cotton curtains, laying a golden quilt on my bed. I hear Father crossing the landing, then the rasp of his razor as he shaves, singing a Gaelic song. He is secretary of the Games and he knows that everything is ready on the field above the town. The marquees that came on the cargo boat have been erected; the latrines dug. He rinses his razor under the tap and I hear the Old Spice I gave him for his Christmas being slapped on. Mother is now up, going down to the kitchen.

I go to the corner of my bedroom and lift up the two swords. They have authentic looking hilts, but the blades are made of silver-painted wood. I cross them on the carpet and lace up my pumps. Today I am dancing at the Games, and this year I hope to win the sword dance. I have been practising all winter, making the floor of my bedroom vibrate, with Mother claiming that the ceiling in the sitting-room will come down on top of her as she watches a soap on our temperamental set which sometimes has to be slapped to restore the signal. But Father came up to watch me dancing, sitting on the bed as I danced by the window over my dud swords.

'I'll be amazed if you don't win it this year, Marsali.'

It's Games morning and I'm practising, landing on my toes as softly as possible to save them for the competition. Soon Mother will call up that breakfast is ready, but I will eat nothing more than a brown egg because I have seen competitors in previous years throwing up behind the marquee.

I know where Father is. He is at the sitting-room window, watching for the dark blue bow of the steamer to slide up to the pier. It left one of the islands in the dawn and is packed with spectators for the Games. Many of them are Father's customers in the bank, but that isn't why I hear the door closing as he goes down to the pier to wait by the gangway. It's for the pleasure of hearing the Gaelic of another island spoken. I have put my swords away and can see the first of the spectators coming along the street from my high window. The men have raincoats folded over their shoulders and caps pushed to the backs of their heads as they look into the window of Black the ironmonger's. Their stout wives are at the other window where knitting needles are crossed in balls of wool.

The procession up to the field musters* at the memorial clock and is led by the laird with a plaid over his shoulder and a long stick. The pipe band behind him is followed by the spectators, going up past the aromatic wild roses on the back brae. But I am already on the field, my number pinned to my frilled blouse. I have on my pumps and am practising in the subdued coolness of the tent, using my swords. Mothers are fussing round other competitors, straightening the pleats of kilts and exhorting them to dance as well as they can.

A girl comes in. She is pretty, with a blue velvet bonnet angled on her blonde hair, and a plaid, held at her shoulder by a cairngorm brooch, trailing at her heels. She is carrying a holdall that says Canadian Pacific, and in her other hand she has two large swords.

'Hi.' she says to us all, and comes across to the corner of the tent where I am exercising to make my toes supple. 'I'm Jeannie Maclean.'

I go into my bag and check the programme. There is no such name down for the sword dance. She sees me looking at her quizzically and she says: 'I'm a late entry. Mom posted the form a month ago but it never reached here. I went to see the secretary and he says I can compete since I've come such a long way.'

'Where are you from?' I ask.

'Saskatchewan.'

Immediately that name takes on a romantic resonance and I want her to say it again.

'It's in Canada,' she informs me, lacing up her pumps. 'We have wheat fields that go on for miles.'

---

*musters: gathers

I am trying to imagine the ripe golden crop waving in the breeze when she adds more information. 'Our people came from this island.'

'From here?' I say, surprised.

'U-huh. They were cleared last century and they found their way to Saskatchewan. They did pretty well. We have four combine harvesters on our farm and my father has a herd of Aberdeen Angus he shipped across.' It's not a boast but a factual statement.

'Are these real swords?' I enquire, reaching across to touch them.

'Claymores. My folks brought them across from this island. My grandfather said we fought with them at Culloden.'

'If they came from here they must have spoken Gaelic,' I say.

'Sure, but we lost it when we intermarried. My great-grandmother was a squaw. I'd love to learn Gaelic.' (She pronounces it Gale-ick.) 'Do you speak it?'

I nod, but I'm getting too involved in this conversation instead of preparing for the competition. She, after all, is a rival, and as she lays the swords on the turf and begins a practice dance, I see how good she is. She's dancing as she converses with me, her shadow turning on the canvas wall of the tent. 'I've been doing this since I was three, first with two wooden spoons on the floor of the kitchen. I need to win today. Mom's outside.'

I don't want to stay in the tent to watch her practise because it's undermining my confidence, so I go over the hill, past the latrines, already busy with early drinkers, to a quiet hollow where I lay down my swords in the hum of insects and make my own music with my mouth to dance to. But I feel there is something lacking. My feet are heavy and I am aware of the clumsiness of my hands above my head. As I turn my foot touches a blade, and I stop, upset.

I hear Father's voice through the megaphone calling the competitors for the sword dance. As I go back over the hill I feel he has betrayed me by letting the girl from Saskatchewan – I am beginning to hate the name – enter for the competition when the rule says entries in advance. The dancing judges from the mainland are sitting in the shade of a lean-to beside the platform, with paper to mark the competitors on the card tables above their knees. I sit on the hill to watch, but I am not impressed by the standard.

'Number 79, Jeannie Maclean.'

She comes up on to the platform with her swords under her arm and there is a confab among the judges. Yes, she can use her own swords, as long as the steward lays them down. He makes them into a cross for her on the boards. She puts her hands on her hips and bows to the judges as the pipes tune up. I see from the first steps what a beautiful dancer she is. I am watching her toes and they hardly seem to touch the boards, springing in the air above the blades, now touching a diced stocking. The people around me on the hillside are enthralled. To my left there is a woman also wearing a Maclean kilt, with a cape. She is standing, holding up her thumbs to her dancing daughter.

Jeannie Maclean is turning in the air, her kilt swirling. She is twenty seconds off the trophy which is waiting in a table in the secretary's tent. Four nights ago I watched father polishing it, and he told me: 'Your name will be on this, Marsali.'

Jeannie Maclean is performing her last movement when she comes down, heavily. I see the side of the pump touch the blade which slices through the leather. She is lying on the boards, holding her bleeding foot, and her mother is shouting behind me instead of going down to her injured daughter. 'You damn fool!'

Father calls for Dr MacDiarmid through the megaphone and he comes in his Bermuda shorts with his medical bag. Jeannie Maclean is helped off the platform and hops to the first-aid tent, her hand on the doctor's shoulder, to have her foot stitched.

It's my turn to dance and I turn to bow to the judges in the lean-to. How dearly now do I wish that the trophy for the sword dance was going across the ocean to Canada, to sit in a glass case in a prairie house where Gaelic was once spoken. But Jeannie Maclean is out of the competition. As my toes touch the boards I am dancing to the refrain: Sas-katch-ew-an, Sas-katch-ew-an. I see Father crossing the field, his secretary's rosette on his lapel. He has come to watch me and he stands, smiling in encouragement. I know I have never danced better because this is a performance for him. Sas-katch-ew-an, Sas-katch-ew-an. I am reaching for the sky. Mother is on the hillside waving but she has never really been interested in Highland Dancing or Gaelic because she's from the mainland.

I can feel my toes so sure, as they come down between the blades. I turn to face my father, my knuckles on my hips. This is for you, Father, for all the patience and love, for the Gaelic words you give me. I turn to face the marquee. I can see a slumped shadow on the canvas, another shadow hanging over it, an arm raised. This is for you, Jeannie Maclean, with your wounded foot, your treacherous swords and your angry mom. I have nothing but pity and love, and as I bow to the judges and the applause rises I know that one day I will go to Saskatchewan.

The Hamecomin

Sheila Douglas

The overnight bus decanted Al and his luggage at the foot of the Horse statue in the High Street, where he stood blinking in the early morning greyness like an astronaut who had just landed on the moon. He couldn't have felt more of a stranger there, thousands of miles away from the familiar skyscrapers and crowded streets of Toronto, yet this was his home.

He looked up at the figure of the man on horseback, bearing the tattered standard, a ghost from the past, and reflected that he might just as well be thousands of miles away as well, for all the relevance he seemed to have to the here and now. '*You* were actually glad to get back here,' he reflected. 'Not like me at all.'

When he'd fallen out with the old man more than ten years before, he'd taken a job in Canada and honestly thought he'd never set foot in Hawick again. But here he was and, worst of all, only a few days before the Common Riding, the part of his past life he never wished to live through again: especially the last one, the occasion of the worst quarrel with his father, the day he lost his girl and all the honey of life turned to gall, amid all the surge of warm feelings around him, the crowds, the horses, the flags and himself outside it all, not part of it. The memories were too bitter.

So why had he come back? That was something else that was hard to think about. Only a month ago his brother Rob's letter arrived with its harsh news: their mother had been diagnosed as suffering from inoperable cancer and had been given only a short time to live. If he wanted to see her, he'd better not waste any time. Al had loved his mother with a fierce, unspoken love and she was the only one he'd really missed, although he'd have been loth* to admit it. 'I'll be over as soon as I can make arrangements to have my affairs looked after,' he promised on the phone.

---

*loth: reluctant

'Aye, aye,' said Rob, who had an awesome idea of his brother's business responsibilities. 'Ee canna jist drop aathing an rin.'

If only Rob knew! Al's electronic business, like his marriage, had disintegrated the year before, washed away in a flood of alcohol. The reason he wanted to play for time was to make sure he'd really dried out. The Forrester Centre had been an enormous help, but Al felt it was early days to try out his new-found sobriety in what he remembered as a fairly hard-drinking neck of the woods, particularly at this time of the year. He'd actually forgotten about the date of the Common Riding until Rob reminded him and by then he'd booked his flight. Fate seemed to be conspiring to put him to the test.

He was in no hurry now to phone Rob to fetch him up to the farm. He sat down on a bench in a little paved area off the deserted street, lit a cigarette and contemplated again the victor of Hornshole on his exhausted horse. Strange how the memory of a victory could bring tears. Into his mind cane the half-forgotten strains of the lament for Flodden:

The flooers o the forest are aa wede awa.

How they loved to relive the past, these people he'd grown up amongst, and what a hell of a grim past it was! No good old days in the Borders. He'd been glad to get away from that as much as from his father's thrawn* intransigence. Now here it was again, confronting him.

As he sat there, the town was beginning to waken to the early morning: a few people began to walk past on their way to work; a milk float clattered its bottles; paper boys sped by on bikes; cleaning ladies went by in twos, laughing stridently. Then he saw a dumpy woman, walking a dog, stop and try to light a cigarette from a lighter that wouldn't work. She wore a grey cotton jacket and a tired yellow headscarf, her feet in cheap sandals. Al automatically got up and flicked his own lighter, and she raised a tired expressionless face to him. 'Thenks,' she said, and lit her cigarette before walking on.

---

*thrawn: stupid, stubborn

Al looked after her without much interest, for she was hardly worth a second glance, when she stopped to look back along the street, not at him, but at something else. Her profile stirred his memory. He'd a feeling he'd known her once. Before he could dredge up a name to go with the face, she was on her way again. No doubt there'd be many faces he'd see like this, that belonged to the old days, drab, dour faces maybe he'd been glad to forget. A clock chimed nearby and he thought he'd better phone the farm. Rob would have been up for at least two hours by now. He found a phone box and felt strange dialling the number without the international code before it.

'Hirselfit*,' came Rob's voice on the line, a strong Border voice.

'Rob?'

'Aye. Is't yow, Sandy?' Rob still used the name Al had grown up with, but discarded in the city across the Atlantic, where he thought it made him sound like a hayseed and also tended to attract other expatriate Scots, whose acquaintance he'd no desire to cultivate. 'Whaur ir ee?'

'In the town,' replied Al. To everyone in the area that meant Hawick. 'By the statue,' he added.

'Did ee faa oot o the sky?' asked Rob in amazement. He'd been expecting to drive to Glasgow Airport to meet Al's flight from London.

'No, no. I took an overnight bus.'

Rob was even more nonplussed. Why should Sandy, who could well afford it, choose not to fly from Heathrow? 'Weel, jist haud on. A'll be doon for ee in haf an oor.'

Al replaced the receiver and went back to his bench, a little reassured. There'd been no hint of hostility in his brother's voice, no hidden resentment – because Rob had never understood Al's antagonism to his father – just a straightforward acceptance of the fact that he was there. He should have known that Rob would be above the narrow-mindedness that had caused his father's enmity. The old man had just wanted things to go on the same way for ever, and be done as

---

*Hirselfit: Hirselfoot, a fictitious farm near Hawick

they had always been done by the same people for the same reasons. He couldn't see that it just wasn't possible. Al didn't want to be a sheep-farmer and wasn't prepared to shackle himself to that way of life when it wasn't his choice, and his father couldn't understand that. More than anything it was the quarrel with his father that had made him hate the Common Riding, because it also sought to perpetuate the past. Even with his father three years dead the hatred still rankled. He wished he could have come home at any other time of year but this.

Hawick was now humming with life around him and he was being eyed curiously by some passers-by for his smart luggage and his fine city suit.

'Hey mister,' called one wee lad in a Ninja turtle tee-shirt, 'ir ee a Yank?'

'Nope.'

'Ir ee an Aussie?'

'Definitely not.'

'Where ir ee fae then?'

Al looked down at the cheeky face and grinned. 'Believe it or not,' he said, 'son, I'm a Hawick callant*.'

The boy made a derisive noise. 'Leyin bugger!' he shouted, aiming a kick at one of Al's expensive leather cases as he ran off. Al laughed ruefully. How could he feel annoyed at the boy, when he'd spent the last ten years trying to forget he'd ever seen the place. He didn't look or sound as if he belonged there. He deserved the insult.

Minutes later a landrover drew up and Rob leapt out, taller and broader than ever, tanned and moustached just like the old man. He grasped Al's hand in a crushing grip and slapped his shoulder with the other hand, nearly felling him.

'Sandy, man, it's guid ti sei ee!' he cried; then, staring at his brother's face, he added, 'But what ails ee? Ee're lookin puirly!'

Boozing and the break with Marianne had left their mark on him but he didn't want to let Rob know all that. 'Bitch of a journey,' he said. 'I'll feel better tomorrow.'

---

*Hawick callant: male native of Hawick

'What in hell possessed ee ti come bi bus?' Rob wanted to know. 'Ee could easy hev flown ti Glasgow or Edinburgh an A'd heve met ee.'

'I know. I – had business in London and it was handy for the coach station.' Al lied without batting an eyelid. It was a habit he'd had to acquire. He couldn't tell Rob he'd taken the bus to save money. Rob was under the impression that he was stinking rich. Well, he had been for a few years, but that was over now.

Rob put the cases in the back of the landrover, running an admiring hand over the smooth leather. 'Best o stuff Sandy, eh?'

Al nodded and climbed into the passenger seat and soon they were speeding out of the town, into the bare, rolling hills.

There was something about the Newcastleton road that had always got to Al, a feeling that there was a lot there below the surface that was not seen or heard but nevertheless exerted an influence. He had never been able to describe it or identify it, but now it seemed crystal-clear to him. Perhaps it was because he was now like the road, as he got nearer his old home, with a lot of things scarring his inner self, despite the outward appearance. Rob had spotted this. He hoped to God his mother wouldn't. But that was what was wrong with the road: spectres from the dark and bloody past haunted every inch of it.

'How's mother?' he asked, as the landrover negotiated a hump-backed bridge over a pebbly stream.

Rob shrugged. 'Guid days and bad days,' he replied. 'Ee'll sei an awfi change in her.' He wrenched the gear lever savagely to hide his anger. Al understood. Why should a woman who'd worked hard all her life for her family, toiled on the hill at lambing and dug sheep out of the snow in winter, be struck down in this way? His heart was filled with dread as they approached the steading.

The farm hadn't changed at all while he'd been away, although to Al it looked much smaller than he remembered it. Living among the multi-storey blocks of Toronto had altered the scale of his vision. The landrover rattled into the yard and stopped. Al followed Rob into the kitchen, where their mother sat by the fire, happed* in a warm quilt, looking heart-stoppingly pale and thin, with a tremulous smile that spilled over into tears.

'Sandy, son!' was all she said. He had to bend over to kiss her and clasp her bony hand, on which there seemed to be no flesh left. In the old days she would have been up and putting on the kettle for tea with scones she had just baked. 'Ee've come hyim ti ride the Common!' she whispered rapturously. Al looked at Rob, but guessed from the fierce warning in his eyes that this was the charade he had to play. He smiled and nodded and stroked her hand, not knowing what to say next.

Rob's wife May bustled in from the scullery with a tray piled high with home-baking and a shining silver teapot. 'Ee'll be ready for this, Sandy,' she laughed, as she got the cups and saucers from the dresser.

Al had to admit the smell of home-made bread and pancakes was irresistible. May shook his hand warmly and touched his cheek with hers. 'Oo're glad ti sei ee!' she told him. 'Ee've been away owre lang!'

Rob was at his cabinet, taking out the whisky bottle. 'A dram, Sandy.' It was a statement, not a question. The crunch had arrived.

'Not for me, thanks, Rob.'

'Eh?' Rob couldn't believe his ears. 'Sorry, Sandy, what did ee say?' In spite of himself he was nettled.

'I said, not for me, thanks. I don't drink any more.'

'Dinna – ?' Rob stood, bottle in one hand, glass in the other. 'Is't the truth ee're tellin iz?'

'It is.'

'Bloody hell!' exclaimed Rob. 'Nae wonder ee're luikin sae puirly.'

Al nearly laughed at the irony of this. He'd looked a lot more poorly before he kicked the habit. But Rob would never understand that in a hundred years. 'These pancakes are great!' he told May by way of diversion. Rob sat down and sipped his dram, trying to work out what had happened to his brother.

---

*happed: wrapped up

'And how's eer wife keepin, Sandy?' asked May, as she refilled his teacup, her bright voice wounding him like a knife.

'Oh, she's quite well,' he replied, not looking at her, realising that it was going to be hard to keep up the evasive answers in the face of this warm directness. Lies and secrecy had never played a part in his family's life: blazing rows and confrontations, yes, but they never hid things from one another.

'An the bairns?' smiled his mother eagerly. 'Ir they weel? Hae ee ony ither photies o thum, Sandy?' Round the walls hung the family pictures, including his own wedding photograph and one of his children taken five years ago. The children were now with Marianne. He hadn't seen them for several months because of his spell in the clinic. 'They're doing fine,' he assured her, and took out his wallet where he kept their photographs. His mother seized on them avidly and looked at them for a long time. 'Jamie looks like yow,' she commented, 'but Christina's like her mother.'

Although she's never seen them, she knows them, their names and their faces, he reflected. They mean a lot to her, her grandchildren.

'I wush they were here wi ee,' she sighed.

Al said nothing, but found himself wishing the same. But he wasn't fit, Marianne had told him, wasn't fit to be a father.

'What about your two?' he asked Rob. They'd been born before he left, a sturdy pair of boys.

'Threi,' grinned Rob proudly. 'Mind oo hed another yin? Hei's caaed efter you.'

Al's conscience smote him. How could he forget? Young Sandy would be seven now.

'They'll be back fae the schule later on. On the bus, mind?'

Al remembered the rattly old school bus, threading the hill roads, sun or snow, with the noisy bunch of country bairns. These were happy memories but they gave him as much if not more pain than the sad ones. All of a sudden he couldn't stand the room any longer, the claustrophobic family circle, his mother's wasted face, the questions, the photographs. He rose to his feet. 'I think I'll go for a walk up the hill,' he announced.

Rob and May exchanged a glance of delight. They obviously thought he was keen to see the place again, tread the old paths and look over the flocks at pasture. All he wanted was to get away from them.

'A'll pit eer cases in eer room,' called Rob after him. 'It's aye there yet, ee ken!'

That's just what he was afraid of.

Al took the winding path that led up to the rocky outcrop they used to call the Spy Rock, because it looked out over the whole valley. They could see people coming on the road from either direction and they could also look to the back of the hill. Al sat down on it as he'd often used to do as a boy, and for a few moments it was as if time stood still. Nothing seemed changed, until he looked across the valley and saw the black blight spread across the hills: sitka spruces in their thousands, planted in huge square blocks, disfigured the green rolling slopes. Down below him he saw the head waters of the Liddle reduced to a trickle, limping down the valley among what at one time had been underwater rocks, now exposed like bald heads to show how the stream had shrunk, robbed of its life by the thirsty plantations.

'Fine day,' said a voice at his back, and looking round he recognised, almost in disbelief, the tall erect figure of Henry Wilson, his father's old shepherd, stick in hand and dog at heel, looking at him sternly.

'Henry!' he exclaimed in surprise, for he hadn't expected him to be still living.

The craggy face broke into a smile. 'I didna ken ee, Sandy,' he said. 'When was't ee came?'

'Hardly an hour ago,' Al told him.

Henry grunted and pulled on his pipe. He never had much to say, but when he did it was usually to some effect. Never use a dozen words when two will do, was his motto.

'How old are you now, Henry?' Al couldn't help asking, for the shepherd had seemed quite elderly to him even when he was a child.

'I'm eyty-twae,' was the reply, without a hint of either boast or complaint.

'You should be retired, surely?' Al said in wonder.

'How? There's naethin wrang wi iz,' retorted Henry. Al looked at his strong frame, healthy face and long-striding legs, and had to admit that a lifetime on the hill did not seem to have taken its toll of him, as he'd seen life in the city do to men twenty years younger. Suddenly he wanted to confide in this ageless man – like a rock that weathered all the storms –and speak of all the things he couldn't mention down there in the farm kitchen, where all the warmth of family, the imminence of death and his mother's unbearable smile seemed to call in question so many things.

'Henry,' he began. But then he couldn't find the words to go on.

'Ee'll hev a lot ti think aboot,' said Henry, almost as if reading his mind. 'Tak eer time. It's no an easy raw for ee ti hoe.' Al realised that he didn't need to tell Henry anything, explain anything. He began to understand a remark he'd heard years ago, maybe from his father, that you couldn't spend your years on the hill without learning wisdom. 'Tak eer time,' repeated Henry. 'Sei yon stream doon there.' He pointed with the stem of his pipe to the struggling Liddle Water. 'It wis greed that dune that an aa. It hez a gey hard time gettin doon ti the Holm. But it gets there. Mind ee, it needs the Hermitage Witter ti help eet on, like. Aye, it'll be aye here efter we're weel away.'

As they stuid there quate like twa auld freens*, Al refleckit on whit the herd had said an ferlied* at his smeddum*. It wis like a draucht frae a spring well efter the wershness* o the life he'd left ahint in Toronto, the jiggery-pokery an the preisures he'd tholed* for sae lang. Mair's the peety he'd tane the wrang gait oot there. For the first time, he wis gled he'd had jist eneuch siller* ti traivel hame.

---

*freens: friends
*ferlied: marvelled
*smeddum: wisdom
*wershness: dullness, sourness
*tholed: endured
*siller: money

'Thanks, Henry,' he said, at the feenish, 'I'll need ti be away doun, noo.'

Henry noddit an strade awa, wi the lang, rollin herd's gait, whusslin on his dug as he gaed awa ti tent his yowes*.

Al gaed back doun the track ti the ferm, hummin an air he couldnae pit name til, but efter a few meenits he launched as it cam ti him whit it wis – the auld Common Riding sang* that steered the bluid o Hawick men:

Teribus and Teriodin
We will up and ride the Common

Whit in creation had brocht that ti mind?

When he cam ti the kitchen door May's voice caaed oot, 'Rob, ir ee there?'

'No,' he answert, gey near withoot thinkin. 'It's Sandy.'

He went ben the room ti fin his guid-sister wi the district nurse, red-heidit ablow her blue cep an a face that brocht back the past in a bleeze. Isobel Elliot – her name wis in his mou jist as if he'd never forgotten it.

It wis an unco* thing but the sicht o her an the memories didnae seem ti hurt noo.

'Hallo, Sandy,' she smilit, as if it wis nae mair than ten days instead o ten years sin they'd seen ane anither. 'A'm sorry A wisnae right wakin when A seen ee in the toon.'

'Sorry?' He wis slow in the uptak.

'It wis yow, wis eet no, that gien iz a light? A wis walkin the dog in the High Street.'

'Wis it yow, then?' He wis thunnerstruck. He'd seen his childhood sweethairt an thocht it wis some dreich*, ill-faured,

---

*yowes: ewes
*sang: song sung at the Common Riding, the annual Hawick festival derived from the old custom of a procession to confirm the town boundry. The meaning of 'Teribus and Teriodin' is obscure but may derive from a Norse warcry.
*unco: strange
*dreich: dreary

nameless woman he micht hae seen somewhaur afore. Whit wis wrang wi him?

'A'm no at my best early in the mornin,' she chirmed. May didnae jine in the joke. Her face wis wan an dowie*.

'Sandy,' she said. 'Mum's gey hard up. She'll hev ti gaun ti the hospital.'

'When did it happen?' Sandy wis bumbazed*. He'd been up the hill for nae mair nor an oor.

'Oh, she can take a bad turn gey quick,' May said. 'She's been hingin on jist ti see ee. Now ee're here, she's happy.'

They gaed intil the bedroom whaur his mother wis as white as the bedsheets unner the blue quilt.

'She's hed her pills, an the doctor'll gie her an injection. She's in nae pain. The ambulance'll no be lang.'

Luikin doun at her face, he kent she wis deein. A terrible knot o dule* fankled* his kist, forcin oot his braith. Toronto seemed no jist thoosans, but millions o miles away fae him noo.

---

*dowie: serious
*bumbazed: confused
*dule: grief, misery
*fankled: caught up

Relationships

Mossy

Audrey Evans

Miss Stone had her departure from the school nicely planned. At one minute to four, she lined them up. Ten seconds before the bell, she sent a boy to spit his bubble-gum into the wastepaper basket. Then she dismissed her very last class. They walked demurely down the corridor, then roared off round the corner. Miss Stone, a complacent smile on her neat, blunt features, picked up her coat and briefcase, and nipped across the corridor into the Detention Room.

There, studying the Detention Book, was Mr Downie, youngest and newest teacher on the staff.

'Mr Downie,' she said. He jumped, and Miss Stone smiled grimly.

'As you know, I retired from teaching at 4 pm today.'

Mr Downie appeared to be at a loss.

'You're not having a party, then?' he said.

'Certainly not. The Rector being unctuous*, concealing how much we dislike each other; other members of the staff who were once pupils here – an incestuous situation, don't you think? – would recall how I once belted them. No thank you. Now, I would like – '

'I was once a pupil here,' said Mr Downie, 'and you belted me.'

'Indeed? I didn't realise. But then I have never involved myself with my former pupils.'

'You weren't much interested in your current ones.'

Miss Stone's eyebrows rose. Mr Downie was evidently made bold by the prospect of her departure.

'I'm sorry I haven't time for a stroll down Memory Lane,' she said. 'I have a favour to ask of you. If you would be so good – '

'If I would be so good! Always the soul of courtesy, you were. Till there was trouble. Then it was a hand like a breeze

---

*unctuous: oily, ingratiating

block rearranging your brains. I think you impaired my hearing permanently.'

'Then I must speak louder. I would like to take your Detention, this evening.'

There was a bewildered silence.

'You mean do my Friday night Detention for me?'

Miss Stone sighed and waited.

'Why? I mean . . . I've been lumbered with it all term, and nobody's ever agreed to swop with me. Who would? Dammit, it's Friday, isn't it? And,' he went on, marvelling, 'you wouldn't be swopping if you're leaving today – '

'Mr Downie,' said Miss Stone, losing patience, 'I wish to avoid certain contingencies. Such as the medium sweet sherry, now awaiting me as a surprise in the Ladies' Staff Room. Another is having my hand shaken warmly by colleagues whom I have detested for years. In short, I want to hide until everybody has gone home. Will you assist me?'

Mr Downie grinned broadly.

'You should have been called Stony, not Mossy,' he said. 'You always had your own way, didn't you? I wish I had the knack. The kids terrify me.' He glanced down at the Detention Book and shuddered. 'Especially the girls. One thing I always appreciate, though – your sardonic* sense of humour.' His own humour overcame him. 'OK, sister,' he said, 'you talked me into it.'

Miss Stone waited, looking down her nose.

'Yes, yes, thank you. I'll do it,' he said, his hand furtively covering his ear.

Left alone, Miss Stone settled at the teacher's desk, and had a look at the Detention Book. Only two names. She set her briefcase on the desk and opened it. Then her face went blank. It was a shock, slight but cutting, to realise that she had no correction to do. She liked to have work in hand when she was supervising a class. Then, if there was any disturbance, she could look up, severe and preoccupied. It gave her, she felt, an advantage.

---

*sardonic: bitter

She sat, red pen tapping the desk, surveying the little room, designed to depress further pupils who were already in disgrace, from beige walls to buff ceiling and brown floor. It was like sitting inside a parcel.

Outside, in the corridor were footsteps and voices, and the harsh, dangerous shouts of boys. They gradually died away. She wished with a fervour that surprised her, that somebody would come in.

The door opened, and a small, very dirty boy edged round it. He came and stood at the desk. He didn't look round the room or at Miss Stone. In fact, he gave the impression of not looking anywhere. His eyes were as blank as marbles.

'You're . . . let me see . . . Wayne. Is that right?'

'Aye.'

'Here's your work.'

She handed him a booklet and a sheet of paper, and he wandered off to a seat. He took some time to settle, pulling out a pen, then a pencil, and looking at them as if he had no idea what to do with them. Then he opened the booklet and began to write, slowly and carefully, squinting along the paper, his head lying along his arm.

The door burst open. The girl's face sagged in disappointment when she saw who was sitting at the teacher's desk.

'Aw!' she said. 'Mossy! I mean – sorry, Miss Stone. Where's Mr Downie?'

'I am taking Detention tonight,' said Miss Stone, in her colourless voice.

'But Mr Downie – he always takes it on Friday.'

'Looking forward to seeing him, were you? I see it was he who set you the Detention. Sit down, please.'

The girl slumped into a seat. She was about fifteen, pretty in a heavy, moist sort of way. The boy, Wayne, had not raised his head, but wrote steadily on. The girl's flushed face looked as if it might turn resentful and truculent*. Miss Stone moved in, with the ease of long practice.

---

*truculent: aggressive

'What is your name? Ah, yes. Dawn. So, Dawn, you made yourself obnoxious in Mr Downie's class. He gave you Detention. And you were hoping to be alone at last with him, give or take one or two other numbskulls, was that it? Well, I am sorry to disappoint you. Mr Downie wished to see his fiancée this evening, and I agreed to take his place.'

'Fiancée!' The foolish mouth dropped, the eyes filled with tears. Dawn took the sheet of paper and sat, blinking and sniffing, making no effort to write.

'Go on,' said Miss Stone. 'A 500-word essay on Good Manners. And mind you write in paragraphs.'

Miss Stone sat, erect yet relaxed, hands clasped in front of her. She felt as she usually did, completely in control of the classroom situation. Then she was annoyed to realise that she was consciously achieving that control by an effort. 'For goodness' sake,' she said to herself, 'what's the matter with you? Another half hour and you can send them home. Then you can get away, as you planned.' She thought of her austerely comfortable little flat, and the glass of fine dry sherry she had promised herself.

It was no good. She was rattled. Why? It wasn't that silly girl, now sighing heavily as she considered the concept of Good Manners. No. It was the boy. There was something incongruous in the contrast between his dirty clothes and close-cropped hair, his plastic jacket and heavy laced boots, and his earnest, scribe-like endeavours.

She went over to him. He laboured on, entirely absorbed in his work. He was copying from a booklet called *Spelling for Primary Schools*. There were lists of short, easy words . . . 'able, ache, adder, affair'. His writing began large and ungainly, then trailed uncertainly upwards. Some of the words were wrongly spelt. She looked hard at the boy.

'What class are you in, Wayne?'

'2B Special, Miss.'

'How old are you?'

'Fourteen, Miss.'

She picked up his paper.

'Let me have a look. Good. That's very good, Wayne. "April" has a capital letter, though.'

'Oh, aye,' said Wayne, and resumed his task.

'How many of these are you supposed to do?'

'Fifty.'

'You've done far more than that. You can stop now. I'll put your work on the desk for Mr Price. He'll be pleased with you.'

She put out her hand for the piece of paper. To her surprise, he snatched it up and held it to him.

'I want tae dae mair words,' he said.

'No, no.' She was patient, in an impersonal way, because he was one of Mr Price's lot, in 2B Special. 'You've done enough.'

She stood, waiting or him to obey, but he sat, head bent, clutching the creased sheet of paper.

'Can I no dae mair words?'

Miss Stone was silent, puzzled.

'I like daen them!' His voice was suddenly loud and rough with defiance, and Dawn glanced up.

'I can dae it. You said I was daen it guid. I'm guid at it.'

He laid his paper on the desk, and smoothed it out.

Miss Stone opened her mouth to say something so sarcastic that it would sweep Wayne and his spelling list out of the Detention Room and out of her life for ever. But she did nothing of the kind. It was as if a veil had been wrenched aside, and a hard clear light shone on this dirty little boy. For the first time, in the long, cold years, she understood something . . . what he was saying . . . what he was telling her . . . why he was clinging to his pathetic task, so awkwardly done . . . that he was finding peace and satisfaction in the work. He was happy that he could cope. Everything in his school life was a fog of misunderstandings, a jungle of blundering errors, with no track to follow. Here, with his little book and his sheet of paper, he was like everybody else, successful and safe.

The moment of vision, with its pity, passed. To reassure herself, Miss Stone said, with a shaky laugh, 'You're not supposed to enjoy Detention, Wayne. You'll undermine the whole system.'

He sat silent, accepting yet again that he never knew what teachers meant.

Then he said, 'It's guid, this.' He gave a strong shiver. 'It's fine and warm, here. Quiet.'

He wiped his nose on his sleeve and began to write again.

Miss Stone became aware that Dawn was staring, mouth half open. She knew, by pupil instinct, that a teacher had lost control of a situation.

Miss Stone decided to get rid of her.

'Have you finished, Dawn?' she said.

'Here, no Miss,' said Dawn, startled.

Miss Stone went to look over her shoulder.

'It'll do,' she said. 'You can finish it next Friday, when Mr Downie's here. I'll make a note of it in the Detention Book.'

'Oh, great.' Dawn got to her feet. Then her face darkened.

'I didna know that Mr Downie was engaged.'

'Did I say that? I must have been mistaken.'

'He's not engaged?'

'Not at all. He is, in fact, still looking for his ideal woman. Better luck next Friday, Dawn.'

She watched the girl making ready to go, clumsy and excited, like a puppy. She felt amused contempt for her, and an admiring awareness of her own malice and her . . . what had Mr Downie called it? . . . her sardonic humour.

At the door, the girl turned. She smiled radiantly, her face lit with love and joy.

'Thanks, Miss,' she said. 'You're great.'

Miss Stone felt that her moment of self-congratulation had been quite spoiled.

Left with Wayne, Miss Stone prowled round the Detention Room. While this wretched child was doing his Detention so conscientiously, *her* professional conscience directed that she should wait a little longer, even though all sound had died in the corridor and the Staff Room sherry would be long re-corked.

She glanced again at the Detention Sheet. Docherty . . . Docherty . . . a boy with the same shape of head and the same bristly fair hair.

'There was a Kevin Docherty,' she said.

Wayne jerked upright, and the pencil fell from his hand.

'That was my dad, Miss,' he said.

'Miss What?' said Miss Stone, from force of habit.

'Miss Mossy.'

She shot a keen glance at him. Too stupid to be trying it on. He didn't look cocky; in fact, he was watching her almost as if he were frightened. Then his glance slid sideways.

'You tellt my dad once he was as thick as a dry stane dyke.'

'Did I? I must have been annoyed with him. What's he doing these days?'

'Nothing,' said Wayne. He hesitated, blinking rapidly, then said, 'My mam was in that class.'

'Oh? What was her name?'

'Janet.'

'What was her maiden name?'

Wayne looked blank.

'Her name before she married your Dad.' Wayne shook his head.

'Janet,' mused Miss Stone, ' . . . Janet Stewart . . . That would be it, eh?'

'Dinna ken,' said Wayne.

'That would be in 1970. No, no, that would mean that Janet was only fifteen – ' She stopped, embarrassed. There was no reaction from Wayne. He picked up his pencil, ready to start that interminable copying.

'Have you any brothers or sisters, Wayne?'

'Twa brithers. Twa sisters.' He began to write again.

Miss Stone reflected on Wayne's parents. Although she always claimed she couldn't remember a thing about her ex-pupils, she had excellent recall. Janet Stewart, a wee fair girl, and Kevin Docherty . . . She remembered him all right. Big hands curled into fists, blue eyes congested with sullen hatred, while she stood over him, raking him with a sarcasm against which he had no defence except whispered obscenities. She had beaten him under, but only just. One of those boys whose violent fate has been decided and who are destined to decide the fate of others. Poor, silly wee Janet. Fifteen years old. She hadn't stood a chance. Miss Stone shrugged off Janet and her like.

'Your father was a bit of a hard man when he was at school. Did you know that?'

'Aye,' said Wayne. Then he whispered, 'He batters me. And my mam.'

Miss Stone recoiled in alarm and distaste. Serve her right for showing interest. It was time the boy went home.

'Wayne, you've done two whole sides. Now, off you go.'

He didn't move. Sitting on the edge of her desk, her patient tone becoming ragged, Miss Stone said, 'Wayne, look, this has been my last day in this school. I don't teach here any more. I want to go home. And you must go home, too.' She took the booklet and paper from him and placed them on the desk. He watched her, picking at a filthy thumbnail. With a return of that eerie clarity of vision, she saw how white his face was, how hollowed his eyes.

'Get rid of him,' she thought. 'He's trouble. Don't ask him any more questions. You're on your way home . . . get him and yourself out of this room, out of this school . . . '

It was too late.

'I canna go hame. I'm feart. I want to stay here.'

Dreading the answer, Miss Stone had to ask.

'Why are you afraid?'

'It's my dad.'

It took ten full minutes to get the story out of him. At the end of it, Miss Stone sat back, appalled.

The father had beaten the boy and his mother repeatedly. The other children were in care. Last night, things had been very bad. The woman and child had crouched in the kitchen, listening to Docherty in his drunken frenzy, raging above them. In the morning they had crept about, thinking themselves safe for a while. Then Wayne's father had flung open the kitchen door. The heavy, thudding blows on his mother had driven the boy beyond reason. He had picked up a heavy iron coal-shovel and struck at his father.

'It didna hurt him. It didna! Just his back. But he came at me and he said, "I'll kill you." An' I ran awa, an' he shouted after me, "When you come back the nicht, I'll batter you senseless! I'll kill you!" I was feart to go back . . . I cam tae the school.'

'And you haven't told anyone about this? A teacher?'

'Naw. Just you, Miss.'

Just her. Miss Stone sprang to the Detention Room door and looked the length of the corridor. No one in sight. No one to help. Everyone had done what she had wanted them to do, and gone home, leaving her with a boy, who had gone through a whole school day, half out of his mind with terror at what lay in wait for him at the hands of his father.

'Mam,' said Wayne behind her, 'My mam . . . '

It was growing cold in the Detention Room. Outside, it was darkening, the wind was getting up, and rain was flung against the windows. Distracted, she muttered, 'The police – we could tell them – '

The boy started up in terror.

'No' the police!'

'But somebody must be told – '

Wayne's grimy hand clutched her arm, and even then she shuddered with distaste, because no child had ever dared touch her.

'No,' said Wayne. 'You come wi' me.'

'Come with you? Come with you where?'

'Hame. I'll no be feart if you come wi' me. Please. Please, Miss Mossy.'

Miss Stone pulled her arm free, and went to sit at the teacher's desk. She sat erect, as she had always done, contained and in command. But it was an outward show, a parody. Within her raged tempests of fear and anger.

'It's not fair,' she moaned. 'I've retired . . . I've escaped . . . it's nothing to do with me . . . Why should it be me? I've survived everything because I never *never* got involved – '

The boy stood anxious, at her shoulder, and for a moment she thought she must have cried aloud.

'Come on,' he said, and his face was old with dread.

Miss Stone was beaten at last. Defeated by the enemies she had held at bay so long: pity and, stronger by far, compassion.

She got up, her movements random and slow.

"Where do you live, Wayne?'

'The Valley.'

'Of course,' said Miss Stone, drearily. 'Where else?' Hay Valley Gardens, that septic patch of decaying warrens.

They walked along the corridor. Once, Miss Stone stumbled and nearly fell, for no reason.

'What will I find? Oh, what will I find?' Her mind threw up ranging images of fear and disgust. Kevin Docherty, his great granite hands, his face full of an old hatred . . . and a weeping, beaten woman. Sordid, violent, ugly beyond belief . . . Among the terrors of what was to come, there sounded, as from another world, the voice of Mr Downie.

'I wish I had your sardonic sense of humour . . . you always got your own way . . . '

Wayne looked up into her face.

'You're no' laughin' are you?'

'No. No. Not laughing.'

He put his hard, dirty little claw into her hand. She closed her fingers strongly over it, but it was the boy who drew *her* out into the rain and the wind and the dark.

Napoleon and I
Ian Crichton Smith

I tell you what it is. I sit here night after night and he sits there night. In that chair opposite me. The two of us. I'm eighty years old and he's eighty-four. And that's what we do, we sit and think. I'll tell you what I sit and think about. I sit and think, I wish I had married someone else, that is what I think about.

And he thinks the same. I know he does. Though he doesn't say anything or at least much. Though I don't say much either. We have nothing to say: we have run out of conversation. That's what we've done. I look at his mouth and it's moving. But most of the time he's not speaking. I don't love him. I don't know what love is. I thought once I knew what love was. I thought it was something to do with being together for ever. I really thought that. Now I know that it's not that. At least it's not that, whatever else it is. *We do not speak to each other*.

He smokes a pipe sometimes and his mouth moves. He is like a cartoon. I used to read the papers and I used to see cartoons in them but now I don't read the papers at all. I don't read anything. Nor does he. Not even the sports pages though he once told me, no, more than once, he told me that he used to be a great footballer, 'When I used to go down the wing,' he would say. 'What wing?' I would say, and he would smile gently as if I were an idiot. 'When I used to go down the wing,' he would say. But now he doesn't go down any wing. He's even given up the tomato plants. And he imagines he's Napoleon. It's because of that film he says. There were red squares of soldiers in it. He sits in his chair as if he's Napoleon, and he says things to me in French though I don't know French and he doesn't know French. He prefers Napoleon to his tomato plants. He sits in his chair, his legs spread apart, and he thinks about winning Waterloo. I think he's mad. He must be, mustn't he? Sometimes he will look up and say 'Josephine', the one word 'Josephine', and the only work he ever did was in a distillery. Napoleon never worked in a distillery. I am sure that never happened. He's a comedian really. He sits there dreaming about Napoleon and sometimes he goes out and examines the ground to see if it's wet, if his cavalry will be all right. He kneels down and studies the ground and then he sits and puffs at his pipe and he goes and takes a pair of binoculars and he studies the landscape. I never thought he was Napoleon when I married him. I just said *I do*. Nor did he. I used to give him his sandwiches in a box when he went to work and he just took them in those days. I don't think he ever asked for wine. Now he thinks the world has mistreated him, and he wants an empire. Still they do say they need something when they retire. The only thing is, he's been retired for twenty years or maybe fifteen. He came home one day and he put his sandwich box on the table and he said, 'I'm retired' (that was in the days when we spoke to each other) and I said, 'I know that.' And he went and looked after his tomato plants. In those days he also loved the cat and was tender to his tomato plants. Now we no longer have a cat. We don't even have a tortoise. One day, the day he stopped speaking to me, he said, 'I've been hard done by. Life has done badly by me.' And he didn't say anything else. I think it was five o'clock on our clock that day, the 25th of March it would have been, or maybe the 26th.

Actually he looks stupid in that hat and that coat. Anyone would in the twentieth century.

I on the other hand spend most of my time making pictures with shells. I make a picture of a woman who has wings and who flies about in the sky and below her there is a man who looks like a prince and he is riding through a forest. The winged woman also has a cooker. I find it odd that she should have a cooker but there it is, why shouldn't she have a cooker if she wants to, I always say. On the TV everyone says, 'I always say', and then they have a cup of tea. At the most dramatic moments. And then I see him sitting opposite me in his Napoleon's coat and I think we are on TV. Sometimes I almost say that. But then I realise that we aren't speaking since we have nothing to speak about and I don't say anything. I don't even wash his coat for him.

In any case, how has he been hard done by? He married me, didn't he? I have given him the best years of my life. I have washed, scrubbed, cooked, slaved for him, and I have made sandwiches for him to put in his tin box every day. The same box.

And our children have gone away and they never came back. He used to say it was because of me, I say it's because of him. Who would want Napoleon for a father and anyway Napoleon didn't spend his time looking after tomato plants, though he doesn't do that now. He writes despatches which he gives to the milkman. He writes things like 'Tell Soult he must bring up another five divisions. Touty sweet.' And the milkman looks at the despatches and then he looks at me and then I give him the money for the week's milk. He is actually a very understanding milkman.

The fact that he wears a white coat is neither here nor there. Nothing is either here or there.

And sometimes he will have forgotten that the day before he asked for five divisions, and he broods, and he writes 'Please change the whole educational system of France. It is not just. And please get me a new sandwich box.'

He is really an unusual man. And I loved him once. I loved him when he was an ordinary man and when he would keep up an ordinary conversation when he would tell me what had happened at the distillery that day, though nothing much ever happened. Nothing serious. Nothing funny either. It was a very quiet distillery, and the whisky was made without trouble. Maybe it's because he left the distillery that he feels like Napoleon. And he changed the chair too. He wanted a bigger chair so that he could watch the army manoeuvres in the living-room and yet have enough room for the TV set and the fridge. It's very hard living with a man who believes that there is an army next to the fridge. But I think that's because he imagines Napoleon in Russia, that's why he wants something cold. And on days when Napoleon is in Russia he puts on extra clothes and he wants plenty of meat in the fridge. The reason for that I think is that the meat is supposed to be dead French soldiers.

He is not mad really. He's just living in a dream. Maybe he could have been Napoleon if he hadn't been born at 26

Sheffield Terrace. It's not easy being Napoleon if you're born in a council house. The funny thing is that he never notices the aerial. How could there be an aerial or even a TV set in Napoleon's time, but he doesn't notice that. Little things like that escape him, though in other ways he's very shrewd. In small ways. Like for instance he will remember and he'll say to the milkman, 'You didn't bring me these five divisions yesterday. Where the hell did you get to? Spain will kill me.' And there will be a clank of bottles and the milkman will walk away. That makes him really angry. Negligence of any kind. Inefficiency. He'll get up and shout after him, 'How the hell am I going to keep an empire together with idiots like you about? EH? Tell me that, my fine friend.' Mr Merriman thinks he is Joan of Arc. That causes a lot of difficulty with dresses though not as much as you would imagine since she wore men's armour anyway. I dread the day Wellington will move in. I fear for my china.

Anyway that's why we don't speak. Sometimes he doesn't even recognise me and he calls me Antoinette and he throws things at me. I don't know what to do, really I don't. I'm at my wits' end. It would be cruel to send for a doctor. I don't hate him that much. I think maybe I should tell him I'm leaving but where can you go when you're eighty years old, though he is four years older than me; I would have to get a home help: he doesn't think of things like that. One day he said to me, 'I don't need you. I don't need anyone. My star is here.' And he pointed at his old woollen jacket which had a large hole in it. Sometimes I can hardly keep myself from laughing when I'm doing my shells. Who could? Unless one was an angel?

And then sometimes I think, Maybe he's trying it on. And I watch out to see if I can trap him in anything, but I haven't yet. His despatches are very orderly. He sends me orders like, 'I want the steak underdone today. And the wine at a moderate temperature.' And I make the beefburgers and coffee as usual.

Yesterday he suddenly said, 'I remember you. I used to know you, when we were young. There were woods. I associate you with woods. With autumn woods.' And then his face became slightly blue. I thought he was going to fall, coming out of his dream. But no. He said, 'It was outside Paris and I met you in a room with mirrors. I loved you once before my destiny became my sorrow.' These were exactly his words, I think. He never used to talk like that. He would mostly grunt and say, 'What happened to the salt?' But now he doesn't say anything as simple as that. No indeed. Not at all.

Sometimes he draws up a chair and dictates notes to me. He says things like, 'We attack the distillery at dawn. Junot will create a diversion on the left and then Soult will strike at the right while I punch through the centre.'

He was never in a war in his life. He was kept out because of his asthma and his ulcer. And he never had a horse in his life. All he had was his sandwich box. And now he wants a coronet on it. Imagine, a coronet on a sandwich box. Will this never end? Ever? Will it? I suffer. It is I who put up with this for he never leaves the house, he is too busy organising the French educational service and the Church. 'We will have pink robes for the nuns,' he says. 'That will teach them the power of the flesh which they *abominate*,' and he shouts across the fence at Joan of Arc and says, 'You're an impostor, sir. Joan of Arc didn't have a moustache.' I don't know what I shall do. He is sitting there so calm now, so calm with his stick in his hand like a sceptre. I think he has fallen asleep. Let me put your crown right, child. It's fallen all to one side. I could never stand untidiness. Let me pick up your stick, it's fallen from your hand. We are doomed to be together. We are doomed to say to the milkman, 'Bring up your five divisions', for morning after morning. We are doomed to comment on Joan of Arc's moustache. We are together for ever. Poor Napoleon. Poor lover of mine met long ago in the autumn woods before they became your empire. Poor dreamer.

And yet . . . what a game . . . maybe I should try on your crown just for one moment, just for a short moment. And take your stick just for a moment, just for a short short moment. Before you wake up. And maybe I'll tell the milkman, We want ten divisions today. Ten not five. Maybe that would be the best idea, to get it finished with, once and for all. Ten instead of five.

And don't forget the cannon.

The Lighthouse

Agnes Owens

'Let's go somewhere else,' said Megan to her brother Bobby playing on the beach with his pail and spade. 'Let's go to the lighthouse.'

'I don't want to,' he said, without looking up. At three and a half years he had the face of an angel, but his appearance belied a strong determination to have everything his own way. So thought Megan, aged ten.

'You can stay if you like,' she said, 'but I'm going and I just hope a monster doesn't get you.'

At the mention of the word 'monster' he began to look over his shoulder. It was only recently she'd been telling him about monsters and how they ate children. She'd even shown him a picture of one in an animal book, which was actually that of a gorilla, but it had been enough to make him refuse to sleep with the light off and even with it on he would waken up screaming.

'I don't want to go to the lighthouse,' he said, running over and butting her in the stomach with his head.

'But I do,' she said, skipping off lightly over the sand.

'Wait for me,' he called, picking up his pail and spade and trailing after her.

Together they walked along in a friendly way, going at a pace that suited them both. The day was warm but with a bit of wind. Megan almost felt happy. They came to a part of the shore that was deserted except for a woman walking her dog in the distance. Bobby stopped to gather shells.

'Throw them away,' said Megan. 'You'll get better ones at the lighthouse.'

He emptied his pail then asked if the lighthouse was over there, pointing to the sea wall.

'Don't be stupid. The lighthouse is miles away.'

He said emphatically, 'Then I don't want to go.'

Megan lost her temper. 'If you don't start moving I'll slap your face.'

At that moment the woman with the dog passed by. 'Is that big girl hitting you?' she asked him.

Before he could speak, Megan had burst out, 'He's my brother and I'll hit him if I want.'

The woman studied them through thoughtful, narrowed eyes. 'Do your parents know you're out here in this lonely place?' When Megan said they did the woman walked on with the dog, muttering something under her breath which Megan suspected was some kind of threat aimed at her. She hissed to Bobby, 'See what you've done. For all we know she could be going to report us to the police and you know what that means?'

'What?'

'Mummy and Daddy will be put in jail for neglecting us and I'll have to watch you for ever.'

At that he let out a howl so loud she was forced to put her hand over his mouth.

'Be quiet, you fool. Do you want that woman back?' He quietened down when she promised to get him an ice-cream.

'Where's the van?' he asked, looking around.

'Over there,' she said, pointing in the direction of the lighthouse. At first he believed this, running beside her eagerly, but when they went on for a considerable length without any signs of an ice-cream van he began to lag behind.

'Come on,' she said, 'or we'll miss it.'

'Where is it?'

'Don't ask me stupid questions,' she snapped, thinking how it wasn't fair that she had to be saddled with him all the time. 'You're a silly bugger anyway.'

'I'm telling you swore.'

'Tell if you want,' said Megan, thinking her parents couldn't say much considering the way they swore.

'If you don't come – ' she began, when he started walking again, and just when she thought he was going to act reasonably for once he stopped in front of a rock.

'Look! There are fish in there,' he said.

Grumbling, she went back to investigate. It was true. There were tiny fish darting about a pool of water within a crevice in the rock.

'Aren't they pretty?' she said, just as he threw a stone into the pool causing them to disappear. She shook him by the shoulders.

'You have to spoil everything, don't you?' she said, letting him go suddenly so that he sat down with a thud. But he was up on his feet quick enough when she said, walking backwards, 'A monster's going to get you one of these days, the way you carry on.'

After a good deal of tramping over dry sand that got into their shoes and made their feet sore, Megan suggested they climb up over the dunes on their right-hand side to see if there was a better and quicker path that would take them to the lighthouse. He didn't answer. She suspected he was still brooding about the ice-cream, but he followed her which was the main thing.

Climbing the sand dunes wasn't easy. They kept sliding back down. Bobby did it deliberately thinking it was funny. Megan was glad to see him in a better mood. When they got to the top they found they were on a golf course stretching for miles with nobody on it but a man in a grey track suit. He saw them, came over and said, 'Better watch out you don't get hit with a golf ball. It's not safe up here.'

Megan asked him if he was a golfer – she noticed he wasn't carrying any clubs. When he told her he was just out for the day collecting golf balls, she began to wonder if he might be one of those strangers they'd been warned not to speak to.

'Bobby,' she said loudly, 'we'd better go back. Mummy and Daddy will be looking for us.'

'But I thought – ' he began and was cut off by Megan pulling him back down the sandy slope. When he got to the bottom he said that he'd wanted to stay up there.

'It's not safe,' she said.

'Why not?' Then, as if it had nothing to do with anything, he let out a tremendous wail.

'In the name of God, what is it now,' she said, in the same tone her mother used when totally exasperated.

'I've left my pail and spade,' he said, pointing up at the sand dunes.

She felt like strangling him. 'Well, I'm not going for them,' but when he began to wail loud enough to split the rocks, she said she would go if he came with her to the lighthouse.

'I don't want to,' he said, stamping his feet in temper. 'I want to go back to that other beach where Mummy left us.'

It was then she decided she'd had enough of his tantrums. 'Go then,' she said, giving him a shove so that he tottered on blindly for a few steps. 'I don't want to ever see you again.'

When he turned round she was racing along the beach at a fair speed. He called on her to come back, though it was doubtful she heard him above the cries of the seagulls, but even if she had, she probably wouldn't have stopped anyway.

On arriving at the lighthouse, she saw there was no way to get close to it as it was surrounded by water, not unless she waited until the tide went out and that would take hours. Sullenly, she looked up at its round turreted shape thinking it was much more boring from this angle than it had seemed from a distance. She wished she'd never come. The sea was stormy now with the waves lashing over the rocks. The whole venture had been a complete waste of time and energy, she decided. Suddenly her attention was riveted to what looked like a body in the water. For a split second she thought it was Bobby, which would have been quite impossible considering the distance she'd come. Nevertheless, it was a great relief to discover this was only a mooring buoy. She laughed at her mistake then began to feel uneasy. She could picture him stumbling into the sea for a paddle thinking it was all shallow water. It was the kind of stupid thing he was liable to do. Panic swept over her. What if something terrible happened to him? She should never have left him like that. Without another thought for the lighthouse or anything but Bobby, she began running back to where she'd left him, praying that he'd be all right.

From a distance she saw him hunkered down, digging in the sand. He must have gone up the sand dunes to get his pail and spade after all, she thought. She slowed down, her legs tired and aching, then to her dismay she saw the man they'd met on the golf course. He was hovering a few yards behind Bobby poking some debris on the shore with a stick.

'Bobby!' she called out sharply. 'Come over to me at once.'

He either didn't hear this or pretended not to, but the man did. He looked up at her and began to walk smartly in their direction. Galvanised into taking some kind of action, she ran forward to reach Bobby first. In fact she'd almost got to him when she slipped on a stone covered in seaweed and went down, the back of her head hitting off its sharp edge.

Her eyes were staring up at the sky as the man and Bobby crouched beside her. Bobby said, 'You shouldn't have left me. I'm telling Mummy.'

The man pulled him back. 'Leave her alone. She's in bad enough shape.' Then he put his lips close to her ear. 'Can you hear me?'

When her eyes flickered he put his hand over her mouth and nose and held it there for a considerable time. After that he turned to Bobby saying, 'We'll have to get an ambulance. You can come with me.'

Bobby said he didn't want to get an ambulance. He wanted to go back to the other beach.

'All right,' said the man, taking him by the hand and dragging him towards the sand dunes with Bobby protesting all the way. His cries died down when they vanished over the top.

Later that afternoon, a strong breeze sprang up along the shore, lifting clouds of sand into the air as well as the strands of Megan's hair drifting across her face. Seagulls came down to stand on her and poke her with their beaks, then, as if not liking what they found they flew off to the horizon whilst imperceptibly and gradually her body sank into the sand making a groove for itself. A passer-by might have thought she was asleep, she looked so peaceful. But no one came by that day and in the evening when the sun went down she was gone with the tide.

Activities

Activities

All That Glisters

Understanding and evaluation

1 Consider the title of the story and explain how it reflects the theme of the story. How effectively does the author convey this theme?

2 How old do you think the girl is? Give reasons for your answer.

3 Do you find the ending of the story particularly sad? Describe what happens at the end of the story in your own words and say whether you find it successful.

Analysis

The focus of this story is *relationships*. Relationships between characters are often at the heart of a short story – how characters relate to each other and how they behave can tell us a great deal about their inner feelings and motivations.

Read the section in the story from 'The next day the wee wumman let me use the pens again . . . ' to ' . . . then ah fell intae a deep glistery sleep' on page 5, and answer the following questions:

1 How does the author use language to emphasise the contrast between the girl and her father in this section? Find examples and explain whether you find them effective.

2 Images of light, glitter and colour are important in this section. How are these images used to develop the character of the girl?

3 The relationship between the girl and her father is portrayed through description of appearance, description of inner thoughts and through dialogue. Consider the use

of these techniques in this section and suggest which you find most effective.

Group discussion and individual presentation

1 Children 'escape' from their lives in various ways. For example, they may become engrossed in books, they may spend time playing games or they may daydream a lot!

In a group, discuss the different ways teenagers 'escape' and why they might do this.

2 Prepare an individual presentation on an important moment in your life. You should describe an event which brought about a change in you and perhaps in others.

Writing

1 The girl in the story is fascinated by colour, glitter and drawing. Write reflectively about your response to art. Is it important in your life?

2 Write an imaginative story or poem or drama script in which you explore a parent/child relationship.

The Only Only

Understanding and evaluation

1 'Talk was the pastime, talk and work the currency . . . '

The island is a close-knit community. How does the writer convey this closeness?

2 The story is told in the third person and is not narrated, for example, by the mother. Why? Do you find this effective?

3 Consider the title of the story. How does the title reflect the story's theme?

4 Do you find the ending of the story shocking or surprising? (Refer back to the beginning of the story. Does the first sentence give any indication of how it will end?) If so, how is this feeling of shock or surprise created by the author?

Analysis

The focus of this story is *tension*. In a short space of time, the author of a short story must build towards its climax. Careful word choice builds up tension, as can description of the thoughts and actions of the characters.

Read the section of the story from 'In the restful numbed cold silence . . .' to ' . . . and to grow no more.' on page 14.

1 At what exact moment in the story do you think tension begins to build? Quote the word, phrase or sentence and explain the reasons for your answer.

2 Tension builds up throughout this section. Pick out words and phrases in this section which contrast with the stillness and quiet described in the first phrase, 'restful numbed cold silence'. For example, 'churning' gives an impression of vigorous, violent, movement.

3 Are there any words and phrases in this section which suggest what will happen at the end? Quote them and suggest how effective they are.

Group discussion and individual presentation

1 In a group, consider the advantages and disadvantages of being an only child. You may use the story as a starting-point for your discussion if you wish.

2 Prepare an individual presentation about this story – you may concentrate on one aspect, for example, tension, the ending, or you may give general comments on its effectiveness.

Writing

1 Write an imaginative story which has a shocking and unexpected ending.

2 *The Only Only* touches on some of the issues involved in living in an isolated community. Perhaps you live in such a community yourself.

Write an essay in which you consider the advantages and disadvantages of living in a small or isolated community.

All The Little Loved Ones

Understanding and evaluation

1. 'Do you still love me?' and 'What are you thinking?' Does the wife find these questions difficult to answer? Suggest reasons for this.
2. What is the 'precipice' or 'ledge' to which she refers?
3. Which parts of her life does the wife appear to value, in your opinion?
4. How do others view her relationship with her husband?
5. Write a few paragraphs describing the wife's personality, quoting evidence for your answer. Do you feel sympathy for this character?

Analysis

These questions focus on the *opening* of the story. The opening of a short story gives an immediate indication to the reader of the mood or tone of the story, as well as its likely content and theme.

Read the story from the beginning to 'wants me to cuddle up close.' on page 15.

1. The author chooses to start the story with a concise, direct statement in the first person. Why?

   Does this contrast with the style used after this statement? Why?
2. The author makes use of repetition in this section. Quote examples from the extract and suggest why this technique has been used.
3. The narrator is unsure whether to leave her family. Suggest how the style of the opening reflects this. (You might comment on word choice, sentence structure, repetition and so on.)

4 Consider the image of the daffodil. What are the effects of this image?

5 The opening of this story suggests a number of themes, for example, love, escape, family, identity. In your opinion, which of these themes does it convey most effectively? Suggest how the author develops this theme in the opening.

Group discussion and individual presentation

1 In your group, discuss a number of possible reasons for the break-up of the family in today's society.

In conclusion, is divorce ever justified, especially when children are involved?

2 Give an individual presentation about this story in which you explore the wife's dilemma. Consider the advantages and disadvantages of her present situation and her options.

Writing

1 The main character in the story loves her husband but sometimes finds this love claustrophobic. She loves her children in a different way.

Write a reflective essay about what love means to you. You could consider your family or a relationship.

2 Write an imaginative story from the point of view of a child, using an appropriate style. You should explore and develop a theme in your writing – you may use one of the themes of the story if you wish.

Fearless

Understanding and evaluation

1 'He was an alkie all right, but not a tramp . . . '

What gives the impression that Fearless might be a tramp? Answer in your own words.

2 How do women and men differ in their attitude to Fearless?

3 Do you find the narrator's eventual reaction to Fearless surprising? Explain your reasons.

4 'But I still hear something like him . . . ' Suggest what 'something like him' might be.

Analysis

These questions will focus on *narrative voice*. The narrative voice in a short story is crucial – the author may wish the reader to observe the action and events more objectively by writing in the third person (using 'he', 'she' or the name of a character). The author can make the reader become more involved in the story be describing feelings and emotions directly in the first person ('I').

Read the story from the beginning to 'A bogeyman.' on page 25.

1 What narrative voice is used in the section before 'A bogeyman.'? What are the author's intentions in choosing this narrative voice and what are the effects of this?

2 The narrative voice changes in the section from 'I have to be careful here.' on page 25 to the end of the story. What are the intentions of the author in adopting a new narrative voice, and what are the effects of this?

3 Look at the use of dialogue on page 24. Who is speaking in each case and why have capitals been used? Does this

device have an effect on the reader and do you find it successful?

Group discussion and individual presentation

1 In your group, consider the character of Fearless.

- What is unpredictable about him?
- Why does he behave in the way he does?
- What do the reactions of others tell you about him?
- Do you find him believable?

2 Give an individual presentation in which you reflect on an incident in your childhood which at the time seemed frightening but which, on reflection, might be considered humorous.

Writing

1 Write a poem, story or drama script in which aggression is the main theme. You should take care to convey the reasons for this aggression.

If you are writing a story, pay particular attention to narrative voice.

2 Write a discursive essay on the topic of vulnerable people in our society. Should we care for those who cannot care for themselves in residential homes or should such people be integrated into the community and, if so, how?

You should undertake some research into social issues before presenting the arguments and reaching a conclusion.

Feathered Choristers

Understanding and evaluation

1 What types of disruptive behaviour does the boy display in school? (Summarise these in your own words.)

   Can you suggest reasons for this behaviour?

2 Why do you think Billy has invented his imaginary Martian friend?

3 The boy is at the bottom of the class while the Brains is at the top of the class. Find references to the boy's intelligence and to his position in class. What evidence is there to suggest he is not as stupid as the Mad Ringmaster or his teacher believe?

4 The boy becomes increasingly confused. Find five examples of this and explain each of them in your own words.

5 Look at the list below. Which aspects of the story do you find realistic and which do you find unrealistic?

   - Billy's imaginary Martian friend
   - Billy's disruptive behaviour
   - Billy's dislike of poetry
   - The Mad Ringmaster's behaviour towards Billy
   - The teacher's behaviour towards Billy

Analysis

These questions will focus on *structure*. The structure of a short story can vary according to plot and theme, but it will always be tightly controlled because of the brevity of the genre.

Read the story again, paying particular attention to the structure.

1 The story is written as a series of conversations. How does the author begin and end each conversation? What effect does this have?

2 Look at the structure of each conversation. Do the conversations follow a pattern? If so, describe this pattern.

3 Compare the first conversation with the last section. How are they different and why?

4 What are the effects of writing the story as a series of radio transmissions? Suggest why the writer has used this device.

Group discussion and individual presentation

1 In your group, discuss Billy's personality. Find examples of his mental instability and suggest reasons for his state of mind. What future do you think he has?

2 Give an individual presentation in which you describe an imaginary friend you invented in childhood. Avoid a simple narrative account by structuring your presentation in an interesting and challenging way and include insights and reflections about your creation of this friend.

Writing

1 Write a reflective essay about a time when you thought you were treated unfairly at school. Consider the most effective structure and narrative voice for your writing.

2 The main character in the story behaves in a way which may appear unstable to others but which he describes rationally.

Write about how you behave. Might your behaviour seem irrational to others but perfectly normal to you?

Striker

Understanding and evaluation

1 How is Luke educated in 2035? Below is a list of typical aspects of education today. Explain in your own words how these are different for Luke:

teachers	registration/assembly	blackboards
homework	playground	classrooms
pupils	books	

2 How do Luke's feelings about the Cyberstation change once the game starts?

3 'He had never kicked a baw in his life.' What does the final sentence of the story tell you about life as a teenager in 2035?

4 Did you find the story difficult to understand? Why? Do you think the use of dialect is effective? Give reasons for your answer.

Analysis

These questions will focus on the *language* of the story. The type of language used – colloquial, slang, informal, formal, simple, complex, humorous – can be important in expressing theme and revealing character. It is also crucial to the mood or tone of the story.

Read from 'He'd been up tae hi-doh aw moarnan . . . ' to 'Luke quit the hoose.' on page 42.

1 Luke's mother uses ' . . . mealie-moothed NewCal English . . .' whereas Luke prefers 'Auld'. Looking closely at what the characters say, explain what these terms might mean.

2 Suggest what the mother's attitudes are to a) the past (symbolised by the 'Auld' language) and b) the present.

3 Part of the humour of the story lies in the author's use of contrast. Find examples of contrast from this section and suggest how the humour is created.

4 The language used is in a conversational tone. What does this contribute to the story and do you find this device effective?

Group discussion and individual presentation

1 In a group, discuss how much you would enjoy living in 2035. Which aspects of Luke's life would appeal to you and which would not?

2 You may speak with a strong Scottish accent, you may use a dialect, you may speak with a completely different accent from those around you.

   Give an individual presentation in which you explain the importance to you of the way you speak. You could consider how you feel about your accent, how others react to it and whether you would ever consider changing the way you speak.

Writing

1 Write a story in a dialect with which you are familiar.

2 What do you think life will be like in 2035? Write an essay in which you explore the lifestyle of the future.

   You could include descriptions of education, transport, housing, family life, sport and leisure, or any other aspect of your choice.

Rupert Bear and the San Izal

Understanding and evaluation

1 What three books has the child been given? Which ones appeal to the child? Can you suggest reasons for their appeal?

2 The title contains a contrast between an imagined character in a comic book – Rupert Bear – and a domestic, potentially dangerous liquid – San Izal. Are there other examples of contrast in the story itself?

3 'The lack' (page 54). What do you think the child 'lacks'?

4 'I had no words.' Explore the importance of words and/or reading in the child's life.

5 Is the child in the story male or female? Give reasons for your answer.

Analysis

These questions will focus on *theme*. The themes or underlying messages of a short story must be conveyed within a short space of time.

Read from 'The Rupert book was lying open . . . ' to ' . . . to the blade.' on page 53.

1 In what ways does the child's environment differ from the setting of the Rupert book?

2 Can you suggest why the child feels like dying while looking at the 'shining globe'?

3 The child is depressed and negative – find examples of language from the section which reflect this.

4 Look at the list of themes on the next page. Choose which ones you think are themes within the section.

Support each of your choices with a quotation from the text, and explain in your own words why you have suggested it as a theme.

loneliness	poverty	childhood	jealousy
searching	imagination	love	happiness

5 Choose one phrase or sentence which you feel is central to this section because it sums up the theme. Give reasons for your choice.

Group discussion and individual presentation

1 In your group, consider the main character.

- Do you sympathise with the character?
- Do you find him or her believable?
- Why is the character so unhappy?

2 Give an individual presentation about a favourite book or story from your childhood. Do not simply recount the story, and structure your talk carefully – you should explain in detail why the book is your favourite.

Writing

1 In your opinion, how should the question of poverty (either local, national or international) be addressed? You should undertake some research into the subject before you start writing.

2 The main character in this story considers the concepts of God, Heaven and death. Write an essay in which you explain your beliefs about any one or all of these concepts.

Saskatchewan

Understanding and evaluation

1 Marsali appears to be confident of winning at the beginning of the story. How do her feelings change after she meets Jeannie?

2 Marsali's father and Jeannie's mother behave very differently from each other. Look through the story to find out how these two characters behave.

Copy the adjectives below into two lists – one list of adjectives which apply to Jeannie's mother and one list of adjectives which apply to Marsali's father. After each adjective, give evidence for your decision in the form of a quotation from the story.

supportive	uninterested	proud	disappointed
ambitious	angry	jealous	confident

3 'How dearly do I wish that the trophy . . . was going . . . to Canada.'

Why do you think Marsali wants Jeannie to win the trophy so much?

4 Do you think that Marsali and Jeannie want to win for themselves or for other people? Give evidence for your answer.

Analysis

These questions will focus on the *setting* of the story. In this particular story, the writer describes in detail the setting where the action happens. This contrasts with other places mentioned.

Read the story again from 'I know where Father is.' to 'Do you speak it?' on page 59.

1 Find and quote any description of the island setting from this section. In your opinion, what is the author's attitude towards the island?

2 Pick out examples of words or ideas from this section which are specific to Scotland, e.g. 'laird', 'Gaelic'. Suggest why these have been used.

3 Why do you think the name 'Saskatchewan' seems romantic to Marsali?

4 What does Jeannie explain about her family's emigration? Why do you think the author includes this information?

Group discussion and individual presentation

1 In your group, discuss what it means to be Scottish. Consider the following points:

- Where were you born?
- How would you define being 'Scottish'?
- Do you consider yourself to be Scottish?
- Do you think some Scottish stereotypes exist?
- Are you proud of being Scottish? Why or why not?

2 Give an individual presentation in which you describe a competition, race or contest in which you were involved. Try to explain your feelings and reflections in detail, using visual aids where appropriate.

Writing

1 Write an essay in which you discuss what changes you would make to improve the lifestyle of young people in Scotland.

2 Marsali is clear that one day she wants to visit Canada. Write an essay on your hopes and dreams about travelling in the future.

The Hamecomin

Understanding and evaluation

1 'Lies and secrecy had never played a part in his family's life.'

What secrets does Al hide from his family?

What reasons for his secrecy and his reluctance are we given in the story?

2 What does Al realise while talking to Henry? Do you think he changes at this point?

3 Al meets Isobel in the early morning and again at the farm later. Suggest how and why he treats her differently on these two occasions.

4 Suggest a theme for the story, giving evidence for your choice. How effective do you find the ending in terms of the theme you have chosen?

Analysis

The language used by the author – word choice, tone, sentence structure and so on – greatly influences the mood of any short story.

These questions will focus on only one aspect of the language used in this story – *word choice*. As well as contributing to mood, word choice can help to convey the theme as well as 'tell the story'.

Read the story from 'Al remembered the rattly old school bus . . . ' to ' . . . to tent his yowes.' on page 71.

1 In the first paragraph of this section, the writer describes how Al feels about the room. How does he feel and what words are used to convey this? Comment on their effectiveness.

2 On Spy Rock, what words does the author use to emphasise the change in the landscape since Al was

young? Is this a negative or a positive change, and how does the choice of words help you to work this out?

3 '. . . this ageless man – like a rock that weathered all the storms – . . . ' (page 70).

Explain this image and suggest why the writer has chosen it.

4 Why do you think the author has chosen to narrate the story in dialect at this particular point? How effective do you find this technique?

Group discussion and individual presentation

1 In your group, discuss whether you think it is possible to leave your home completely. What are the advantages and disadvantages of living away from home?

2 Give an individual presentation in which you describe the importance of family. You may include ideas about your own family and your place within it. You could also consider the effect of any changes on the family.

Writing

1 Al's family are unaware of the reasons and circumstances behind his return. Write a story or drama script in which the main character is at a turning-point in his or her life of which other characters are unaware.

2 Write an essay about your home town. What local traditions are still celebrated? Are you involved in these traditions or do you avoid them?

Mossy

Understanding and evaluation

1 What does Mr Downie tell us about how Mossy treated him as a pupil? Make a list of quotes as evidence, for example, 'You always had your own way, didn't you?'

2 Look at the words below and choose which, if any, refer to Dawn and which refer to Wayne. Copy them into a table like the one below –

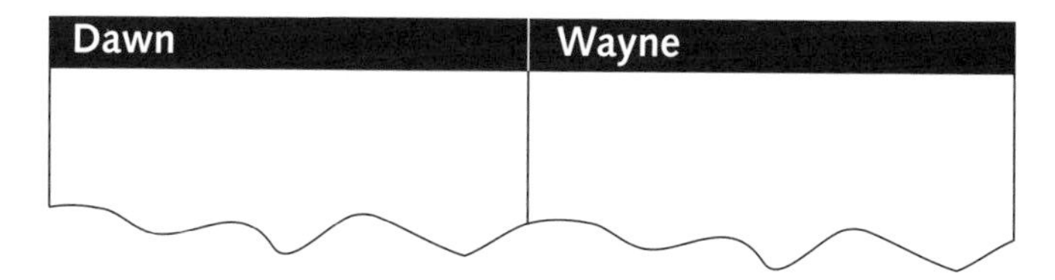

Dawn	Wayne

cheeky unhappy infatuated polite
successful clever shy unloved aggressive

3 What do we learn about Wayne's home background? Answer in your own words and suggest why you think the author has included these details.

4 What do you think will happen to Mossy and Wayne on the way home? Try to bear in mind the characters' personalities and the fact that it is an important day for Mossy.

Analysis

The focus of this story is *character*. The character of Mossy is central in this particular story. Through direct description, her own speech and her reactions to other characters, the reader builds up a picture of a character at a turning-point in her life who comes to a sudden realisation.

Read from 'It was too late . . . ' on page 82 to the end of the story.

1 'Everyone had done what she had wanted them to do . . . '

Look at what Mossy says (to Wayne or to herself) in this section. Quote any examples of conversation which show that Mossy is uncertain and no longer in control.

2 The writer describes Mossy's physical appearance and behaviour. Quote examples of this. What does this tell you about Mossy at this point in the story?

3 ' . . . I never *never* got involved – .'

Mossy feels a number of emotions after Wayne has explained his story. Explain what these emotions are (quoting evidence for your answers).

Group discussion and individual presentation

1 In a group, discuss Mossy's good and bad points as a teacher. Discuss what qualities you feel are necessary to be an effective teacher.

2 Give an individual presentation about the career you would like to follow and your hopes and ambitions for it.

Writing

1 Write a story which starts with the last two sentences of the story. You may use the characters introduced here or create your own.

2 Write reflectively about a teacher who has helped or supported you in some way.

Napoleon and I

Understanding and evaluation

1 The husband in this long-married couple is under a delusion that he is Napoleon. Read the description of Napoleon below. Explain in your own words whether you feel the husband and Napoleon are similar.

> Napoleon had an outstanding military career. In 1814, he tried to commit suicide after a disastrous campaign in Russia but essentially remained a megalomaniac (someone with a mental illness with delusions of grandeur, power and wealth). He was convinced of his own physical and mental perfection, believing himself to be right at all times.

2 'I think he's mad.' Do you agree?

3 The author uses the voice of the wife to narrate the story and describe her husband. What effect has he achieved by using this technique?

4 What surprising suggestion does the wife make at the end of the story? What does this suggest about her?

Analysis

These questions will focus on *description*. In a short story, description – of character, setting, action – is as important as narrative or dialogue in conveying information to the reader.

Read the story from 'He is really an unusual man.' to 'Unless one was an angel.' on page 88.

1 The story is written as an interior monologue, which means that the reader is given only one perspective on the action – the wife's.

How effective do you find this as a means of conveying character and setting? Are you convinced by the wife's account of the situation?

2 Part of the humour in this extract derives from the description of imaginary historical events placed next to description of everyday domestic objects or ideas – for example, ' . . . the meat is supposed to be dead French soldiers.' Quote as many examples as you can find of this technique in this extract. How effective do you find the humour elsewhere in the story?

3 The wife's love-hate relationship with her husband is described in detail. Explain what you think is meant by the phrase 'love-hate relationship' and quote examples of this from the extract.

Group discussion and individual presentation

1 In a group, discuss whether you think the relationship in the story is believable. Consider the different ways in which relationships can deteriorate and suggest reasons for this.

2 Give an individual presentation about marriage. Is it old-fashioned and unnecessary, or is it the ideal context for a committed relationship in which to bring up children?

Writing

1 Write a story or poem based on a relationship which has deteriorated.

2 Write an essay, imagining that you are in a position of power – locally, nationally or internationally. How would you use your power? What changes would you make?

The Lighthouse

Understanding and evaluation

1 Consider the character of Megan. At times, she behaves like a spoilt child; at other times she is caring towards her brother.

Draw a table like the one below and find evidence of how she behaves in different ways. You may quote from the story or explain in your own words.

Jealous	Childish	Caring	Angry

2 The man in the grey suit is not described in great detail – why not? Why is he not given a name? What makes Megan uneasy about him?

3 Find any information you can about the parents of Megan and Bobby. What kind of parents do you think they are?

4 Megan and Bobby are both young children in a vulnerable situation. In the first few pages of the story, which character seems more at risk, and why? Did you find it surprising that both Megan and Bobby became victims of the man?

Analysis

The focus of this story is the *ending*. The ending of a short story sums up some of the elements of the story itself – for example, a shocking ending can come after tension has been built up; a surprising ending comes when the reader has been led to expect a different conclusion; an ending can give a final explanation of a character's actions.

Read from 'On arriving at the lighthouse . . . ' on page 93 to the end.

1 In the paragraph beginning 'On arriving at the lighthouse . . . ', what does the writer tell us about the lighthouse and its shape? Does the lighthouse live up to Megan's expectations? Find evidence for your answer.

2 What does the writer tell us about the sea? Why?

3 Do you find the mood of the story more serious when Megan thinks Bobby is in the water? Give evidence for your answer.

4 Megan is described in the last paragraph as ' . . . asleep, she looked so peaceful.' Do you feel sympathy for her?

Group discussion and individual presentation

1 In a group, discuss the story. Read the statements below about the main character and decide whether you think they are true or false.

- Megan is jealous of Bobby.
- Megan does not look after Bobby properly.
- It is Megan's fault that the man abducts Bobby.

2 Give an individual presentation about a day you spent at the beach in your childhood.

Writing

1 Write a personal reflective essay about your relationship with a brother or sister.

2 Write a poem, drama script or story in which the setting is a beach.

• Word choice.

Suggestions for Critical Essay

1 Basing your answer on at least two stories from this collection, write about the importance of effective openings in short stories. You should analyse the openings in detail and comment on their effectiveness. You may choose similar or contrasting openings.

2 In a short story, one or two characters are introduced and described in a short space of time. Choose one story from the collection and explain how the essential nature of the character(s) is successfully conveyed. You should consider carefully the writer's techniques.

3 The plot of a short story is usually based on one crucial event. Choose one story and show how the author creates tension and builds towards this event.

4 Some of the stories in the collection have features in common. For example, *Feathered Choristers* and *Rupert Bear and the San Izal* both deal with depression, *All that Glisters* and *Fearless* both give a female perspective on childhood.

   Choose a 'pair' of stories and explain in what ways they are similar. Note that you should discuss similarities in the writers' techniques rather than giving simple narrative accounts of the stories.

5 Choose the story from the collection which you feel is most 'Scottish'. This may be because of its setting, its characters or its themes. Through an examination of all three of these aspects, explain why you think the story could not be set anywhere but Scotland.

The best in classic and

Jane Austen

Elizabeth Laird

Beverley Naidoo

Roddy Doyle

Robert Swindells

George Orwell

Charles Dickens

Charlotte Brontë

Jan Mark

Anne Fine

Anthony Horowitz